FATHERS
AND
SONS

Robert Donkin

Published in Great Britain by

L.R. Price Publications Ltd, 2021

27 Old Gloucester Street,

London, WC1N 3AX

www.lrpricepublications.com

ISBN-13: 9781916887459

“Dedicated to all those who have had difficult relationships with their fathers.”

FATHERS AND SONS

Robert Donkin

Chapter 1

1966

LONDON

IT WAS MONDAY morning; the alarm went off at 7.30 a.m.

Andrew Blake groaned and fumbled for the alarm clock, to kill the intrusion into his sleep, then yawned and stumbled out of bed. After a weekend of socializing and late nights, it was time to return to normality.

Andrew was a successful businessman, who owned a boutique in Carnaby Street. It was the "swinging 'sixties", he was twenty-one years old, and although he had recently lost his beloved mother to cancer, he was on a high, his business doing well. His late mother had given him a substantial amount of money, which allowed him to purchase the boutique and set himself up. He had a reliable staff, who would display the latest trendy gear in the shop, then open it up to the public at nine a.m., so Andrew could afford to get to work by about ten.

He left the bedroom in his dressing gown, and sauntered through his luxury Kensington apartment to the kitchen. He tuned into Radio Caroline on his transistor radio, and started to sing along to "Paperback Writer" by the Beatles, currently number one in the music charts.

He put some coffee in the percolator and went to the front door to pick up his mail. There were the usual items of junk mail, which went straight into the bin, and two bills, which he would deal with when he returned home from work later, as well as three letters from fashion dealers, which he would take to work and discuss with his staff, to see if there was anything of interest.

However, there was also a letter which immediately caught his eye, with very neat handwriting, in an expensive Basildon Bond envelope; the postmark was local. Andrew was intrigued.

He poured himself his first coffee and sat at the kitchen table to read the letter …

"Dear Andrew,

I think you will be quite astonished to receive this letter! I can well imagine what your mother has told you about me over the years, and therefore I will quite understand if you tear this letter up and wish that you had never received or read it. However, since your mother's death last year, I have felt the need to write to you, as I would like us to be a part of each other's lives.

It would be good, I think, if you were to hear my side of the story. I do not wish to tarnish the memory of your mother in any way. You may be surprised to know that I loved her dearly, right up to the end of her life, and was devastated that she should die from cancer so young.

I think that, as a young man on the verge of your career, there are things we should talk about, as father and son; I feel that there are some important things you should know. My idea is that we could perhaps meet for lunch somewhere and talk in a relaxed manner, in a pleasant atmosphere. You may be surprised to learn that I have followed your journey of life from the day I left home. I have learned with great interest about your education and the beginnings of your career. I could not be prouder of you as my son, and regret that I was not there for all of the important occasions in your life. But there is a reason for that, which you should now know.

If you are happy to meet up, then please ring me at the telephone number below; my secretary will answer. Just tell her who you are and that you would like to speak with your father, and she will put you through to my office. Then, if you are willing, we can set a date, time and venue to meet up, which is convenient to yourself.

As I said, if I don't hear from you, I will fully understand and will not pressure you in any way. However, I sincerely hope that I do.

God bless you,
with very much love,
Jack, your father."

Andrew was stunned as he read the letter.

His mother's words came back to him immediately: *"He was an absolute waster, who kept us short of money and went off with woman after woman!"* Andrew had grown up with this description of his father as known, and to read this letter now was a great shock.

He sat down and read the letter again… and again!

Andrew was a handsome young man, who had enjoyed relationships with many different girls; there was no end of admirers who would love to be in a relationship with him. However, he had never made a stable relationship with any of them, because deep down he was always afraid that any marriage would turn out to be a disaster, like that of his parents. He had instead led a privileged life with his mother Myra, who was estranged from her husband. Money had never been a problem and he had never wanted for anything. His mother had died last year, and he was still heartbroken over her death. And now this!

"I don't know what to do", he said out loud, to an empty apartment.

He sat for a moment, then picked up the phone and rang his uncle.

"Uncle Joe. It's me, Andrew."

"Hello, Andrew, how lovely to hear you. How are you? How's that new business of yours going?"

"Fine; it's really doing well."

"Your mother would be so proud of you, my boy."

"Well, it's due to her that I am where I am today."

"Well, don't forget your own hard work and initiative! You deserve success. What can I do for you, Andrew?"

"Well, I've had a letter from my father!"

Silence…

"Uncle Joe?"

"Yes, I'm here. What does he want?"

"Well, he wants to meet up with me, and give me his side of the story. I am astonished that he seems to know everything about me, even though he walked out all those years ago, when I was a toddler. How could he know all that? It's weird!"

Again, silence…

"Uncle Joe?"

"Yes, I'm here. Has the letter upset you, Andrew? Do you want to meet him, or do you want to ignore it? Now that your mother's dead it might be a good idea to link up with your other parent. I know that your mother would never have allowed it, but things are quite different now. You could at least hear his side of the story – for what it's worth."

"Well, the truth is, I suppose, that I want to meet him. It's just so odd, after all these years. I can barely remember what he looks like, and Mum's words always come back to me."

"Well, it might be good to get it all off your chest: tell him what you think, and what your mother always told you. Then, you can listen to what he has to say and take it from there."

"Okay, I think I'll do that; he's given me his telephone number, so I'll ring his office later. Right now, though, I have to get to the shop."

"Well, I think that's the right thing to do, lad. You won't regret it, I'm sure."

"Thanks for your advice, Uncle Joe. I really appreciate it."

"No problem."

"'Bye, Uncle Joe."

"'Bye, Andrew, and good luck. Let me know how you get on."

"I will, Uncle Joe. Love to Auntie Clare."

Andrew gathered his briefcase, keys and the spec letters which had arrived in the morning's post, and set off in the hot summer weather to his shop.

In the swinging 'sixties, fashion was a money-spinner. Since graduation, he had bought the apartment in Knightsbridge and set himself up in the business in Carnaby Street, with money his mother had given him. When she died, as an only child Andrew had inherited the house and just over a million pounds. She had always told him that her family were wealthy, and her father had left her well off – Andrew never questioned this and enjoyed a privileged childhood, which more than made up for the lack of a dad. However, nothing could ever really fill the gap of a life devoid of a father. There was always that yearning, that curiosity… Why did he leave?

He reached the boutique and greeted his staff, who had opened up at 8.30 a.m. and set out the various ranges of clothes. There were two young members of staff and they were very reliable. The business had done so well that he was in the happy position to think about expanding it – maybe to bigger premises, or even adding another. He could trust his staff with the day to day managing of the shop, allowing him to visit fashion designers and manufacturers, keeping up to date with the latest trends in the world of fashion. He loved the business, and he and his staff took delight in wearing the latest designs to promote their lines.

Auntie Clare, however, had always wanted him to get a job in a bank, or somewhere more stable. "What if all this 'sixties stuff becomes a thing of the past, Andrew?" she had said.

"Well, we'll just have to move on with whatever the fashion of the day is!"

His mother, of course, had encouraged him, and thought it very cool to have a son in the fashion business, especially in Carnaby Street! She was there on opening day, and bought a lot of clothes which were really more suited to a teenager – but Myra could get away with it; she still had the figure and looks of her youth. She was a stunner.

The phone rang in Joe and Clare's house.

"Joe, it's me, Jack."

"Hi, Jack. How are you?"

"Not bad. Listen, I took your advice and have written to Andrew."

"That's great, Jack. Actually, I already know, because he told me; he rang yesterday. I tried to engineer it so that he accepts your suggestion to meet up; it's time he knew the truth."

"I know, but I'm scared, Joe: this is make or break us! It will either mean reconciliation or rejection for the rest of our lives!"

"Listen, Jack, go easy; don't start by telling him what a bitch my sister was, especially considering the circumstances of her death. He only knows her as a loving mother, whom he has lost. Her lies only made him hate you and sympathize with her 'sad lot'!"

"Yes, I know. You're right. What I thought I'd do is start by telling him about the trust fund I set up for him, when she threw me out. He obviously doesn't know about it, because the arrangement I had with Myra was that as soon as he'd graduated and decided upon a career, she would let me know and I would inform the bank manager, who would then write to him and explain that his father had set this up twenty years ago. No such thing has happened."

"I can't understand why she didn't keep that promise," said Joe. "Do you think she was afraid that it would bring Andrew into communication with you?"

"Maybe, Joe. But, your advice is good; I'll start by telling him about the trust fund. Then, only if his curiosity is pricked, will I tell him what a deceitful person she was: her lies, her men and her escapades."

"Yes, if you do it the other way around it's going to look as if you're the wonderful saviour dad, charging in with arms wide open, come to lord it over your bewildered son and hold him to ransom, for believing everything that bitch told him."

Jack laughed. "Okay, I'll take one step at a time. I don't know what I'd do without you and Clare, I really don't."

"Nonsense. That's what families are for."

"But you're more like my brother than my brother-in-law, Joe."

"Well, maybe Myra's sickening lifestyle has thrown us together. Clare also thinks of you as a brother and not a brother-in-law. Let me know how you get on."

"I will. Wish me luck."

Chapter 2

1945

LONDON

"YOU BASTARD! WHY don't you trust me to take control of the finances? Why do you have to set up a trust fund for Andrew? Do you think I'm going to spend it on myself?"

"Well, Myra, you've hit the nail right on the head there: 'trust' is the operative word here and I don't trust you – it's as simple as that! I want to make sure that when Andrew graduates, he has a slush fund that will set him up for life."

"You bastard!"

"How can you be so unkind, after all I've done for you and the boy?"

"That's probably guilt money for your weird behaviour."

"Weird behaviour? We've had this conversation so many times! If you think that setting up a charity for homeless people, helping those in need, caring for people that the system has let down is weird, then I can't imagine what goes on in your corrupted little mind!"

"Perhaps you're having it off with these street people!"

"Only your filthy mind could think up something like that! That's rich coming from you, anyway, with all the men you've had!"

"Just go, Jack. I don't want to see you again!"

"Does that mean you're throwing me out?"

"Piss off!"

"I still love you, in spite of it all."

"Well, I don't love you."

"Did you ever love me? Or was it the money?"

"It was the money, and if you hadn't wasted so much on that stupid charity, we might still be together. All that money you inherited from your father, going to support wasters!"

"It's just as well you don't want me here anymore, Myra; I can't stand to be near you with an attitude like that! You haven't done too badly, by the way; I made you a millionaire!"

"What about the other millions ploughed into that project of yours?"

"It's not a project; it's a charity to help homeless people, most of whom cannot pay the mortgage on their property, so it has been taken from them. They are decent people, and if we didn't have such corrupt politicians, there would be a law to prevent their homelessness; a decent democracy would allow them to keep whatever proportion of the mortgage they have already paid into. Most of these people lived normal lives until things went wrong – the loss of a job, or whatever. You've never had to worry about anything like that, with this house paid for by me, a million pounds in the bank, making interest, and the use of a villa in Spain."

"Don't lord it over me! Piss off and leave me alone!"

"I shall always look out for you, and make sure that Andrew doesn't fall foul of your antics with all of these men."

"Well, at least they are men, and not wimps like you!"

"You could win an Oscar, Myra; your true, ungracious self only ever comes out with me, your brother Joe and Clare! But, to Andrew there's only this loving mother, who's been done down by her husband… Sob, sob…! I can't believe Andrew hasn't seen through you yet! He will though, Myra – one day he will. You mark my words!"

"You dare say anything to him and I'll—"

"You'll what? Kill me? I wouldn't dream of telling him what you're like; it would hurt him too much. But, one day he'll find out for himself."

"Piss off!"

"You can keep the house. I'll be back for my things when it suits me."

Jack left, slamming the door behind him.

The moment Myra heard the car pulling out of the drive, she poured a gin and tonic and rang one of her toyboys.

Chapter 3

1966

LONDON

"HELLO, THIS IS Blake Charity Foundation. How can I help?"

"Oh, hello. I'm Andrew Blake. I wondered if I could speak to my father, please?"

"Oh, hello Mr. Blake. Of course, I'll put you right through."

Bzzzzzz…

"Mr. Blake, your son Andrew is on the line."

"Oh, good. Put him through, Josie, thank you."

Jack waited, nervously.

"Andrew! You got my letter! I'm so glad you've rung! How do you feel about it?"

In a rather cool tone, Andrew replied: "I'm a bit bewildered, to be honest with you, but I think it would be good to meet up. I've given it a lot of thought, and I think that it will do us both good to hear what you've got to say. And you can hear what *I've* got to say about everything."

"That's great, son."

"Don't call me that," said Andrew, icily.

"I'm sorry, Andrew… I know this must all be very strange and bewildering for you."

"You can say that again!"

"How about we meet at La Tasca for lunch, when you've got time? It's discreet, with little private alcove areas, where we can eat and chat without being overheard."

"Fine by me. How about tomorrow?"

"Okay, that's good. I'll book it now. Shall we say one o'clock?"

"Yes, fine."

Jack put the phone down and stared at it for a while. He was shaking, still very nervous, but also hopeful, considering that Andrew had got in touch so quickly; he obviously wanted to know things sooner rather than later.

He booked La Tasca immediately and rang Joe to give him the news.

After the office closed, he returned home and poured himself a large gin. How would it go tomorrow? He went over and over in his mind what he would say to Andrew, thinking always of Joe's advice. He had a sleepless night, worrying about what he was going to say. He imagined various scenarios and came up with a range of responses, should Andrew be angry, bewildered, incredulous or accepting. He prayed that the latter would be the case, upon his hearing the truth.

The next morning seemed to drag. Josie tried to comfort Jack, assuring him that all would be well.

Finally, it was lunchtime.

Jack got to the restaurant early, to get a good seat, in an alcove on the far side of the restaurant; although the place was busy, being very popular, it was secluded enough. He ordered a beer and sat nervously, waiting.

As soon as he saw Andrew enter the restaurant he got up and went to meet him. He held out his hand, but Andrew ignored it, simply saying: "Hello." Jack led him to the table.

Andrew stared at the man before him. He couldn't see any resemblance. He had been expecting an older version of himself. In turn, Jack surveyed the boy and could see where he got his good looks from: he was like his mother. Though, hopefully, not in personality.

Jack smiled nervously and offered him the menu card. After a few awkward silences they started to converse about the menu, making their choices. The waiter came and Jack gave him the order, choosing an expensive red wine. More awkward silence followed.

Eventually, Jack plucked up the courage to explain that when he had left home, nineteen years ago, he had set up a trust fund for Andrew: initially five-hundred-thousand pounds, which by now should have accrued a good amount of interest.

Andrew stared at him in disbelief; he was stunned. "What?!

Why didn't I know about it? Where did you get money like that?" Andrew sounded almost accusing.

"My father – your grandad – inherited a lot of money from his late wife, your grandmother Rebecca. Her family were wealthy jewellers from Berlin, and had made a fortune in the business. Your grandad went into a nursing home some time ago and, when he died, I inherited a huge family fortune: about five million pounds."

"Wow!"

"After he died, I put half a million into a trust fund for you and gave a million to your mother. I also gave some to Uncle Joe and Auntie Clare. I wanted to do something good with the rest, so the bulk of it created a charity, which I set up for homeless people."

"Wait a minute; you gave a million to Mum? She said her family was wealthy, and her father had left her the money!"

"No, Andrew; your other grandad was as poor as a church mouse."

Silence...

"Anyway, Blake Charity Foundation is my business – and yours, too, if you'd care to be a partner."

Long silence...

"This is so much for me to take in," Andrew said, finally. "I mean... I came here with a long list of accusations, ready to throw at you. Mum always made sure that I understood you were bad news!"

"I know, Andrew. This must be a huge shock for you, but let's try and work through it, shall we?"

"Okay... Dad."

"Oh, how I've longed to hear that word!"

"Mum told me terrible things about you: that you were a womanizer; that you kept us short of money..."

Jack laughed and said: "Are you ready to hear my side of the story, or do you want to think about all this and meet up again? Perhaps speak to some of your friends, or have a chat with Uncle Joe and Auntie Clare!"

"No, I want to hear it now, please. I'm confused... but intrigued."

The food arrived and the waiter poured their wine. Then Jack explained everything to Andrew.

He tried to be as gentle as he could, aware that the boy was recently bereaved of his loving mother, and that it would be damaging to suddenly throw a lot of angry sentiments at him. He told Andrew that she was the one who was unfaithful – on more than one occasion – but that he always forgave her, because he loved her. He never kept them short of money, especially after inheriting his father's fortune, giving Myra enough so that she would never have to work again, and would be able to look after Andrew. In the end, Myra threw him out and told everyone it was his fault, and that he was the one having affairs.

He'd bought a villa in Spain, and even paid for her and Andrew to take holidays there. Uncle Joe and Auntie Clare had enjoyed many holidays there, also.

Jack explained that Uncle Joe was disgusted with his sister's behaviour, and that it was he who had kept Jack informed of Andrew's progress in life: his school achievements, the business he had set up, the many girlfriends he had ditched, and so on... Jack now wanted to make up for the past, and hoped that they could put it all behind them, to enjoy a new relationship as father and son.

Again, silence... Andrew had tears running down his cheeks.

"I'm sorry to shatter your image of your mother, Andrew. The important thing to remember is that I loved her to the end, and she was a good mother to you. She loved you dearly, and brought you up to be the fine young man you are today."

Andrew got up and walked over to his father. Then, crying like a baby, he gave the man a huge hug. They held on to each other for a long time. He returned to his seat.

"I can remember the holidays in Spain. She always said it was somewhere she liked to rent every summer."

"Yes, it is a beautiful luxury villa, right on the seafront of Santiago de la Ribera, in the province of Murcia. However, she never had to rent it, ever! All the family has enjoyed time there – even our vicar."

"Oh, Dad, I'm so sorry we have never had a proper relationship! If only Mum had been honest, we could have been father and son so long ago!"

"Yes, I know, Andrew. But she had problems. Our marriage was good for a while, but after you were born it was as if she felt trapped. That's not your fault, and is nothing to do with your personality, because she loved you dearly; it's more to do with domestic ties, which didn't fit in with your mother's idea of living."

"But, with all that money you gave her, she could have hired a nanny."

"Yes, Andrew, but she spent the money on clothes, cars, other men and, of course, you."

"Do you mind if I speak to Uncle Joe about all this? It's a head-full!"

"No, of course not. I was rather hoping you would do that, in truth, so that you would know I haven't made any of this up – she was his sister, after all."

"Okay, I'll go and see him. Then, perhaps we can have another lunch to catch up?"

They enjoyed the rest of their lunch. Andrew told his father about the boutique and his circle of friends, his interests and his hopes and aspirations for the future. Jack was beaming, and inwardly thanking God that things had worked out better than he imagined. He couldn't wait to tell Joe and Clare.

"Well, that was some lunch; I won't I eat for the rest of the day."

"You go and see your Uncle Joe, then get in touch when you're ready."

"I will."

They hugged and held on to each other for a while, before Andrew made his way out of the restaurant. He walked down the street shaking his head in disbelief.

Jack went to the bar, ordered a brandy, which he knocked back in one, and settled up. He walked back to his office elated.

"Blake Charity Foundation. How can I help?"

"Could I speak to Mr. Blake, please?"

"Yes, of course. Who's speaking, please?"

"José."

Bzzzzzzz…

"Mr Blake, there's a person on the phone for you. His name is José."

"Okay, put him through."

"Hello, I'm Jack Blake. What can I do for you?"

"I want my money!"

"I'm afraid we don't give handouts initially; our charity firstly puts people up in accommodation, then we sort out a job and eventually, when everything seems settled, we help find a property to rent with the new income, or arrange a mortgage for purchase, if the income is sufficient."

"I don't mean that, mate! I'm José! Your wife Myra was my mother, and I want my inheritance!"

Jack went silent.

"Hello?"

Still, there was silence... Then, he answered.

"I'm sorry, but you'll have to prove that is true. And it will cost you quite a bit in solicitors fees to do it."

"I won't need a solicitor, mate! Either you give me the money, or I'll tell your beloved Andrew where you got it from!"

"How dare you! I inherited this estate from my late father!"

"Yeah, but where did he get it from? Ask his Nazi family!"

"I'm going to ring off now. I don't want to hear from you again!"

Jack hung up and walked to the cabinet, where he poured himself a large whisky.

His father was definitely not a Nazi; he was an Englishman! He knew that his grandmother was German, but she had died when he was young, years before Hitler came to power. He did have relatives in Berlin, but they only kept in touch now and again: Christmas cards, birthday cards, the odd visit... nothing more. The war stopped all that, and after the war it was assumed that they had all lost their lives in the terrible bombing which brought about defeat, because they were never heard of again. He could remember his father telling him all about trips to Berlin, to see the family. They were not very close, but nevertheless kept in touch.

He remembered his father saying how strange things were. There were these young lads dressed in uniforms – part of an organization called the "Hitler Youth", they were rather like Boy

Scouts… or so it seemed. In fact, Hitler had been very interested in Baden-Powell, and wished to meet him when he was creating the Hitler Youth. Then there came other men, a little older, dressed in brown uniforms; they were referred to as the "Brownshirts" – very thuggish. He told Jack that nobody really took any notice of them in those days. But, of course, that wasn't how things turned out; they changed the history of Europe.

Jack thought hard to try and find a link between that unsavoury part of history and his gentleman dad, but he couldn't. Still, a worrying, nagging, uneasy feeling kept clawing at the back of his mind.

He buzzed through to Josie.

"Josie, the person who just rang, can you dial 141 and see if there's a number for me to ring back?"

"Yes, Jack, of course."

Jack waited patiently, until Josie came back on to tell him that the number had been withheld.

Jack rang Andrew, and arranged to meet him as a matter of urgency.

Chapter 4

1946

LONDON

"I'M OFF TO Spain. I can't stand it here another moment!"

"Just remember who allows you the privilege of living in Spain for months on end! What about Andrew? Who's looking after him?"

"Not you, that's for sure! Joe and Clare are looking after him."

"But he's not two yet, for God's sake!"

"He loves Joe and Clare."

"I love him, too!"

Jack didn't complain any further, as he knew that he would see a lot of Andrew while the boy was staying with Joe and Clare; without Myra the Monster, they would get some prime family time together.

So, Myra headed off to Spain, setting herself up in the luxury villa, on the seafront of Santiago de la Ribera.

Enjoying a gin and tonic on the terrace, she surveyed the beach. Her eyes were drawn to a hunk, sunbathing on his own.

She quickly downed her gin and rushed to the bedroom to change into her bikini. Thank God Franco had lifted the bikini ban! She locked the villa up and strode across the road to the beach, where she settled herself as near as she could to the hunk, without being indiscreet. She complimented herself on her taste in men, as he seemed even more desirable up close than he was from the terrace of the villa. She pondered how she was going to play this. The war was over, Franco was in power and things were changing, but still she knew she would have to behave herself and obey cultural laws.

Her movements had stirred the boy, who was now aware of her presence nearby. She settled down to sunbathe. She could sense the boy's eyes all over her. He was younger than her, but so what? He was stunning!

"Fancy a gin and tonic, gorgeous?"

"Me?"

"Yes, you! I live in there." Myra pointed to the villa, and the boy looked stunned. He couldn't take his eyes off of her, and the temptation was too great; he succumbed.

As he started to put his clothes on, she said: "There's no need of that. Leave them there by the deckchair; nobody will touch them until we come back."

"No, it's not allowed to walk the streets in swimwear."

"Oh, come on, we're only crossing the road. Be quick!"

"Okay."

"What's your name?"

"Antonio."

"Your English is pretty good. How come?"

"My mother teaches English at the school in San Javier."

"Ah, well, she's doing a good job; keep it up."

They crossed the road, Antonio looking furtively left and right, in case of La Policia or the Guardia Civil. They entered the villa and Antonio was immediately staggered by its grandeur: the beautiful Spanish furniture... everything about it spoke of wealth and luxury. *She must be loaded,* he thought.

"Let's go up to the terrace for drinks. Gin alright?"

"Yes, thank you."

"Come into the kitchen. You can slice the lemon while I pour the gin and see to the ice."

The kitchen was magnificent, and Antonio felt his humble abode, a few streets away, very insignificant compared to this.

While he was slicing the lemon, she eyed him up. *Hmm,* she thought, *how delightful! Can't wait to get those Speedos off.*

The gins were prepared. "Okay, follow me."

Myra led him upstairs, through her bedroom and out onto the terrace overlooking the bay. The view was stunning, and they sat and got to know each other.

Myra told him that her family were quite wealthy, and this was their holiday home. Antonio told her about his mother, Maria, and her teaching career. He explained that his father had died when he was a little boy and his mother had brought him up. He worked for a fruit and vegetable distribution company, and one day hoped to have his own business.

Antonio was a little shy and nervous, but allowed himself to be seduced by Myra. She touched his leg and stroked it up and down. He didn't flinch or move, allowing her to continue until he could contain himself no longer, and leaned forward for a kiss. The kiss was passionate, and led to the frantic removal of his Speedos and her bikini.

When they were both naked, they fell on the bed and made love. Well, it wasn't really love – just uncontrollable lust… sex!

After lying in each other's arms for some time, Antonio said: "Can I see you again?"

"Yes, gorgeous. How about tomorrow night? We'll have a meal in one of these restaurants then come back here. How about that?"

"That sounds great."

So began an affair between the unfaithful wife and mother, Myra, and Antonio, who was several years her junior. It lasted the whole of the time Myra spent in Santiago de la Ribera.

Eventually, it was time for her to return to London.

"I'll be back in about a month's time, so just keep a lookout; when you see signs of life here just give me a knock. It'll be great to see you again and catch up."

"Okay, I'll do that. But I wish you didn't have to go."

"I know, sweetie, but I've got family in London. Don't worry; I'll be back."

Myra knew she would not be back next month; Antonio was just another plaything she was already getting tired of. There were plenty more handsome studs on that beach across the road. If only she could live here permanently…

Unknown to her, Joe and Clare were the next family members to shortly make use of the villa; they arrived a couple of weeks later.

They settled in and made their way to a local bar for the *"Menu Del Dia"*: the "Menu of the Day". Clare didn't feel like cooking on that first night, and the food here was so unbelievably cheap.

The restaurant gave them a fabulous view of the Mar Menor, and on such a clear night they could see right over to the Manga Strip. It was delightful, and set the scene for a wonderful holiday.

"I love this place," said Clare.

"Yes, it's fabulous," Joe agreed. "We're so lucky to have use of it. Good old Harry, leaving all that money to Jack; it's turned our lives around."

"I know. And we must persevere in helping him as much as we can with Andrew. Your sister is a real piece of work, I have to say."

"Yes, I know. She's not right in the head since he was born."

After their meal they returned to the villa and opened a bottle of wine, enjoying the beginning of their holiday.

Knock, knock, knock....

"Who on Earth can that be?" wondered Clare.

"I'll go," said Joe.

"Be careful; it might be a beggar."

Joe opened the door and found a young man staring at him.

"Hola. ¿Puedo ayudarte?" *Hello. Can I help you?*

"Hello. I speak English. I called to see Myra."

"Oh, she's my sister, but she's not here; my wife and I are staying here for a couple of weeks."

"She said she would be here soon."

"Did she? That's odd. Well, I'm sorry, but our family shares this villa for holidays, and she's had hers for this year, I'm afraid; I doubt she'll be here again before next year."

"Oh, I see." Antonio could not hide his feelings, his facial expression portraying a mixture of disappointment, disbelief and annoyance.

"When I get back to England I can tell her you called. What's your name?"

"It's Antonio. Yes, please tell her I called, as she told me to, and as I promised I would."

"Vale, Antonio. Adiós."

"Adiós."

"What was that all about?" asked Clare, after he had closed the door.

"His name is Antonio. I think he's someone Myra picked up – off the beach, probably, if I know my little sister."

"Poor boy!"

"Well, he seemed very nice: very polite and Hollywood looks – just like she goes for! She's obviously led him up the garden path – or should I say the villa steps? I will take great delight in telling her that Antonio called and sends his regards!"

"How many others has she brought here?" wondered Clare. "That's the worry."

Antonio walked away miserably. At the beach, he picked up his deckchair, gathered up his belongings and went to a local bar where, feeling dejected, he ordered a drink.

He really liked Myra, and thought it might have been the start of something good. They'd spent nearly every day together when she was in Santiago. However, a feeling he now had deep down made him realize that it would never work: different countries, different cultures, etc…

He made his way home, feeling that he had been used. How could he ever look at that villa in the same way again? He would need to sunbathe on a different part of the beach in future, especially if there was a chance of bumping into her again. How many other men had she seduced? When he got home, he did his best to hide his feelings, because he knew that his mother could read him like a book.

Chapter 5

1944

BERLIN

"RAUS, JUDEN, RAUS!" *(Out, Jews out!)* barked the S.S. officer, in his sinister, black uniform.

The family of Jews was allowed one suitcase each; they were told to pack their most valuable possessions. They quickly did this in a panic, not thinking properly, and trying to roughly cram as much as they could into their cases, as vicious-looking dogs barked at them, and the S.S. officer and his henchmen menacingly harassed them.

Esther, Rueben and their children, Aaron and Rachel, were forcibly thrust into a truck with other Jews. Esther was crying and Rueben was white, silent and distraught. Aaron and Rachel were clinging to their mother, totally and utterly bewildered, both frightened and on the verge of tears.

"No crying!" barked the Nazi. "You will all be deported to a work camp. There you will be rehoused, given jobs and have the opportunity to make a new life for yourselves. Berlin will be free of you filthy Jewish pigs; there's no place for you swindlers and thieves in the Third Reich, the new Germany!"

The neighbours, all good friends with the Goldbergs, looked on from behind their curtains, terrified. They knew that if they went outside and protested, they would be regarded as "Jew lovers", and would follow them into the truck. One close friend, Otto Grüber, sobbed when he saw the way they were herded into the truck, like animals.

The truck picked up more and more families on the way to the train station, until it was almost impossible to breathe in the back. Crammed into the truck, in darkness, they journeyed on. Eventually the truck came to a halt, and the doors flung open.

Once again, the hatred in the eyes of the S.S. men was frightening; their barking, together with that of the dogs, intensified the fear and trembling amongst the victims.

They were unloaded onto a platform, away from the main passenger area, and loaded onto cattle trucks. They were crammed into each carriage, with no space to sit, and had to endure the agony of an endless journey while standing, with only a shared bucket in the corner for their toilet needs, which was emptied occasionally when the train stopped at stations. The smell in each truck was horrendous.

Some people died on the journey, and were thrown unceremoniously out of the truck when it stopped. At each stop the victims begged for water, but none was given; the doors were slid shut, bolted and the train sped off to its sinister destination: Auschwitz. Many poor souls were lost en route.

Two days after the Goldbergs' house had been fumigated and deep cleaned, Captain Von Heindlebern and his family moved in. All traces of Jewishness had been removed; new furniture replaced the old, except for a rather expensive antique German dresser in the dining room, which Heindlebern and his wife rather liked and deemed to be of value. It had been emptied of all crockery, though, Frau Heindlebern declaring that she could not eat off of plates which had been used by Jewish pigs. Like so many other belongings stolen from Jewish families in Berlin, everything was taken to local markets and sold off cheaply, the money going into the coffers of the Third Reich.

That evening, Captain Von Heindlebern and his family enjoyed a sumptuous meal, accompanied by copious amounts of wine, to celebrate occupancy of their new home.

"Papa, why did you keep the dresser? Is it very old?"

"Yes, Hans, it is antique and quite valuable. Do you like it?"

"Yes, Papa. It looks very German. I think the Fuhrer would be very pleased… Heil Hitler!" said Hans, giving the salute.

"Well, it's so heavy we can't move it, so it will have to stay where it is. But it looks fine, doesn't it?"

"Darling, it's perfect," said Trudi, his wife.

"Here's to the new Germany, here's to our beloved Fuhrer, and here's to our new life in our new home!"

They all gave the salute and raised their glasses.

Hans asked: "Who lived here before, Papa?"

"Some Jews; subversives who have tried to destroy the Fatherland. After the treaty of Versailles, they conspired worldwide to keep Germany down, taking all the best jobs and moving money abroad. You must be learning all about that at school? Their punishment is to be resettled in the east, where they can make a new life for themselves, far away from us."

"Yes, Herr Brüner, our headteacher came around every class in school yesterday; he gave us a lecture on the evil Jews. He brought a photograph of the Fuhrer to the Assembly Hall, and replaced the crucifix on the wall with it. He also gave us little books about Jews."

"Did he really?" said Trudi. "I'd like to see that."

"I'll get it for you, Mama."

Hans went off to find his satchel and came back with a little booklet. It contained cartoon characters of Jews, mostly depicted as hideous, giant-sized rats, with a brief explanation of how Jews had destroyed the German economy.

"Oh, look, Friedrik. How funny! How clever!"

They all laughed.

"A big day for you tomorrow, Hans: you are to be initiated into the Hitler Youth."

"I can't wait, Papa. I'm so proud; it's such an honour."

"We're very proud, too, darling," said Trudi, his mother.

They all gave the salute and shouted: "Heil Hitler!"

Chapter 6

1966

LONDON

"DAD, IT'S ME, Andrew. Your secretary said you wanted to meet up for lunch."

"Oh, yes, Andrew. Something has cropped up and I think we need to chat. Can you manage lunch today?"

"Yes, that's fine. What time and where?"

"Shall we say one, at the Criterion?"

"Great, see you there."

Andrew made his way to the Criterion restaurant later that morning, anxious by his father's words that something had "cropped up".

They hugged and took their seats in the restaurant. The waiter quickly took their drinks order and, before they could speak, another came to take their food order.

Finally, Andrew said: "What's up?"

"Yesterday, a young man by the name of José rang. Josie put him through to me and I naturally thought he was a homeless client, seeking help. It turns out that he's your half-brother. He said that Myra was his mother and demanded his inheritance."

Andrew was speechless for a moment. Then, he said: "How on Earth can that be?"

"Well, judging by his accent and the name José, I would say he's Spanish; your mother must have picked up a Spanish boy on one of her trips to the villa, got herself pregnant then done something to cover her tracks. Now, all these years later, we have this mess. That's the only suggestion I can come up with."

"Oh my god, Dad! If I had any doubts about all you have told me about Mum, then this certainly negates them all. It's actually made my grieving process a lot easier, as I'm developing a great distaste for Myra Blake!"

"My boy, just remember that she had problems and needed help. I tried to get her to see therapists, but she would have none of it. In the end, whatever we might think, she loved you and has done a great job bringing up a fine young man."

"I know, but... all this... Who else is going to crawl out of the woodwork?"

"May I suggest that we both meet up with your Uncle Joe and Auntie Clare?"

"Yes, I think that we must. Also, we need some advice on how to deal with this José."

"I'm going to get the charity's solicitors onto that. The only money he can claim is what belonged to your mum, even though I gave it to her, and legally half of that is yours anyway, if it can be proved that he is your half-brother. It's a drop in the ocean of all the money we have, so I'm not worried about it. What I am more disturbed about is the accusation he made."

"Accusation? What accusation? Tell me."

"He claims that my father – your grandad – had a Nazi family in Berlin, and that's where he got all of his money from: Nazi gold."

"That's ridiculous! According to Uncle Joe and Auntie Clare your father was a perfect gentleman. Let's get in touch with him straight away."

Jack telephoned Joe and arranged to call in with Andrew, to chat with him and Clare about the latest developments.

It was a hot Saturday morning when they arrived, just in time for coffee.

Clare let them in and went off to make the coffee, while they made themselves comfortable in the lounge with Joe.

"Well, Andrew, how has all this affected you? I'm sure you must be bewildered by it all!"

"Oh, Uncle Joe, it's a head-full, but lots of things are now falling into place in my mind."

"Such as?"

"Well, all the times I came to stay with you, for a start. Don't get me wrong, I loved that – it was always a matter of great excitement when Mum said she had business to see to and I was going off to stay with Uncle Joe and Auntie Clare – it's just that occasionally I would return home and find one of her business associates in the house. I often wondered why. Now I know: they weren't business associates at all, were they?"

There was silence...

"I always tried to make sure her men had left before I took you home," said Joe, sympathetically. "Many a time I gave her a real talking to that this could not and should not happen."

After another brief silence, Andrew asked: "How many men are we talking about, Uncle Joe?"

"More than I've had hot dinners," said Clare, as she arrived with the tray of coffee and homemade cakes.

"Now, now, Clare, don't exaggerate!" Joe said, sensitively.

"Well," Jack said, "let's just say it was quite a number, and by what we are about to tell you two, it wasn't just confined to this country."

"What?"

Jack then told Clare and Joe about José, and his demand for money. They were aghast, but both clearly remembered the day a young man had turned up on the doorstep of the villa, asking for Myra. Could he be José's father?

They were even more stunned when Jack told them about the accusation of the Nazi connection.

"This is awful! It could put the whole charity foundation in jeopardy, if there's any truth in it," said Joe.

"My father was no Nazi; the very idea is ludicrous! Come on...! He was everybody's absent-minded grandad!"

"I know," said Clare.

"He had relatives in Berlin, as we know. His wife's sister was called Esther, and she probably died during the war; goodness knows if *any* of the family survived the bombing. Dad's wife – my gran, Rebecca – moved to England to find work, long before Hitler came to power and married my father, while Esther remained in Berlin. We only heard from them at Christmas and birthdays; after the war we lost touch. We assumed they had all died."

"Do you still have an address?" asked Joe.

"I think so, somewhere. I'll look for it."

Clare suggested: "What we really need to do is get an appointment with the bank which dealt with your inheritance. Perhaps there's information there as to who left him this money and why."

"Good thinking. I'll fish out some documents that I kept when his estate was handed over to me, after his death. Then, perhaps we can arrange a meeting with the bank manager there. Is that okay?"

They all agreed that was the best way forward.

Later, when Jack had returned home, he searched through his bureau and found an address in Berlin, where his father used to send Christmas and birthday cards to the family there. He also found the documents he had received from the National Westminster Bank, regarding his inheritance. The bank's address was in Manchester, where he had been brought up, and where his father had lived.

Jack rang the bank to make enquiries, and to find out if it was possible to have a meeting with the manager or somebody else. He felt that there was nothing to be gained by being secretive about any of this, so he explained what had happened, and that the family wanted assurance that no scandal was about to emerge, which would put the Blake Charity Foundation at the forefront of national scrutiny.

Jack also couldn't help feeling that if it was Nazi gold his father had inherited, then at least the money was now being put to good use. Helping and housing homeless people seemed rather apt, considering how many families the Nazis had turned out of their homes and murdered.

Chapter 7

1944

AUSCHWITZ, POLAND

"YOU, TO THE left; you, to the right—" barked the S.S. officer.

With whips to hand and vicious, snarling, barking dogs, the whole scene was hellish. Once the cattle trucks were unloaded and the dead carted away, the victims were selected for work if deemed fit enough, or to the gas chambers if not.

Rueben was chosen to work, looking on in horror as Esther, Aaron and Rachel were separated from him. As he tried to protest, he was clubbed with a rifle butt. He staggered, but regained his stand, and respectfully asked the brute who had clubbed him if his family could remain together, as all could work.

The S.S. officer looked at him with hatred, and told him that the women and children would be taken to another part of the camp, for women's work. Rueben replied that his son looked younger than he really was, and could work like a man.

The officer looked at Aaron, then decided he could be allowed to join his father, while Esther and Rachel were marched off with the other women and children, in another part of the camp.

But, it wasn't a place where they could work; it was a gas chamber.

Though Rueben and Aaron were unaware of this, they would soon come to realize the horror of this death camp and the evil, brutality, insanity and inhumanity which rampaged here, in the name of the "Master Race". As time went on, Rueben and Aaron became enlightened as to the fate of their loved ones. The stench from the chimneys in the distance was one of burning flesh. How could a so-called intelligent and intellectual race of people sink lower than vermin? It baffled them.

But, the harsh conditions gave them no time for grief. Rueben became weaker and weaker; after months of back-breaking work, thin soup and the stale, black bread which passed for food, he developed typhus.

It was a system devised by the regime to work the inmates to death. Life expectancy was about six months, on meagre rations and hard work, in blistering hot conditions in summer and sub-zero temperatures in winter. Everyone wore the same pyjama-type uniform, whatever the weather. The Nazis didn't worry about the loss of prisoner workforce, as more and more victims arrived on a daily basis, by the thousands!

Still, Aaron was determined to survive.

Secretly, Rueben had managed to convey to Aaron that he had secured the family fortune from the jewellery-making business he had inherited from his father, and transferred the money to Swiss banks, just as the Nazis were coming to power. If one of them survived this hell, then they should contact the banks concerned.

One day, Rueben collapsed during roll call, when they had to stand for hours, waiting to be counted. He was clubbed and told to get up, but he couldn't. Aaron came forward to help, but was savagely beaten back. When Rueben made it to his feet, he stumbled and fell again. This time the guard beat him to death.

Aaron watched in anger and humiliation, and held back the tears, knowing that he would be punished for crying.

After Rueben had died, Aaron became very depressed, but even more determined to live. Enduring beatings for such crimes as not looking at the ground when spoken to by an officer, or coughing when the commandant was addressing his prey, or speaking to a fellow inmate during roll call; surviving on thin soup and stale bread; working from five a.m. until eight p.m.; sleeping in appalling conditions; wearing thin pyjamas in ice-cold, snowbound conditions; then, in summer, working in blistering heat – despite all of this, remarkably, he lived.

Every moment of every day was hell. He witnessed brutality on a daily basis. Rumours were rife that the Allies were making good progress, and that it would not be too long before the Germans would lose the war. This kept him struggling on, determined to bear witness to the world about what had happened here, and to regain his family's stolen property.

It was nothing to see a prisoner stripped naked, tied to a wooden punishment bench and flogged. The victim would be forced to count the number of strokes. When he lost consciousness, ice-cold water was thrown over him until he was conscious again, then beating recommenced, and the counting started from one again. Very few people survived this ordeal.

Yet, the smell of rotting corpses piled high, of burning flesh from the crematoria, and the filthy conditions in which they had to exist, actually made Aaron more determined than ever to live!

He kept a low profile and did his best not to draw attention to himself, obeying every command and working hard. His youthfulness, he felt, was his ticket to freedom. If only the Allies would hurry up!

Chapter 8

1966

MANCHESTER

JACK, ANDREW, JOE and Clare found themselves in the foyer of the National Westminster Bank in Manchester Piccadilly, where they were seated and asked to wait until called. They would be meeting with the deputy manager who had actually witnessed the transactions as a young clerk, at the time of Jack's inheritance.

"Good morning, Mr. Blake. I'm George Stanhope, the deputy manager."

"Thank you for seeing us. This is my son, Andrew, and my brother and sister-in-law, Joe and Clare."

"Come into my office and make yourselves comfortable."

They seated themselves on sofas and were given coffee and biscuits, as George Stanhope brought out a file, then proceeded to read various documents.

Jack told him all about José and his accusation, explaining that they were concerned; though they had nothing to hide, they certainly didn't want any scandal to hinder the success of the Blake Charity Foundation.

"Well, I have to tell you that the money came from a Swiss bank, and that your father had relatives in Berlin. But, they were Jews. When things became very difficult for them, Herr Rueben Goldberg transferred a substantial fortune to this Swiss Bank. Explicit instructions were given that, if anyone from the family survived the Holocaust, as long as they could provide proof of identity, they would inherit the fortune. There was a list of names: Rueben, Esther, Rachel and Aaron their children – the next of kin... Then, if no one survived, there were an uncle and aunt in England by the name of Harold and Rebecca Blake. Rebecca had moved to England years before and married Harold Blake. Documentary research proved that Rebecca died in 1947. At that time no one else had come forward to claim the fortune, thus your father, Harold Blake, inherited the estate."

"I wonder why my father never told me any of this."

"Well, I imagine he was embarrassed, because the money belonged to a part of his family which had been persecuted, suffered severely, been robbed of a family fortune and died at the hands of sadistic vermin.

"He told me that he had inherited this money from a distant relative. I asked him who it was, and he said it was a relative of his wife, which of course is almost true. However, with his ill health, he was not in a position to do anything about it. We agreed that, after his death – which we knew was imminent – I would set up a charity with the bulk of the money. The only money we did spend was to put him in an exclusive home, where he had wonderful care at the end of his life, but that money came from his own personal investments.

"You can be quite confident that this money is not Nazi gold; it is most definitely a fortune from the Goldberg Jewellery Company, and you can be grateful for the astuteness of Reuben Goldberg, for transferring the money to Switzerland before the going got tough in Germany."

"Phew! What a relief!" said Jack.

"In fact, I'm sure the Goldbergs would be very pleased to know that their money is being used to help homeless people, considering that they were themselves made homeless and lost everything because of these thugs," said Mr. Stanhope.

"Thank you, Mr. Stanhope. You've put our minds at rest."

They said their farewells and left the bank, then went for lunch in a nearby restaurant, where they discussed how to deal with José. Jack felt that there was something deeper to his story than just the demand for money, and anger at Myra.

They were depressed at having learnt the fate of the Goldbergs. They decided it would be a good idea to search the German Holocaust archives, and see what had happened to them. Andrew said he would like to do this.

Shortly after Jack arrived back at the charity office, the door intercom rang and Josie answered it.

"Hello, my name is José. I spoke to you last week and you put me through to Mr. Blake. I would like to see him, please."

"I'll speak to him and see if he's free."

Bzzzzzzz…

"Jack, the gentleman who spoke to you last week is here; he would like to see you. His name is José. Are you able to see him, or should I get him to make an appointment?"

Jack took a deep breath, but decided there was little point in putting off the conversation. "Oh, that's fine, Josie; please send him in."

As he composed himself, José walked in.

Jack was immediately stunned at how very much he looked like Myra – he was a Spanish version of her! There could be no doubt that he was her son.

"Hello, José, I'm Jack Blake. I have to say that I was very distressed by your phone call, your attitude and the accusation you made when you spoke to me last week! However, I have done some research, and while you may indeed be Myra's son, your accusation regarding Nazi gold is false."

There was a long silence, as the two men stared at each other…

José suddenly broke down and started to cry.

Jack hurried over and took hold of him. The young man blubbed in his arms, and Jack felt immediate sadness for him.

"Tell me what this is all about, José. Perhaps we can sort things out."

"Mr. Blake, I'm so very sorry I came across that way on the telephone. I was so full of anger at the way I have been treated since the day I was born! I just wanted to pour out my anger, and you were the most appropriate recipient at the time, I'm afraid."

"Sit down and let's talk."

The two men took a seat.

Jack explained about the family fortune, dispelling the Nazi link. He went into great detail about the Holocaust, in case José didn't know very much about it. Even though Franco was a dictator, ruling Spain at the time all of this happened, and although he had hands bloodied by all of those he had murdered, Jack felt it was important to mention this to José. After all, Franco was an ally of Hitler, and Jack felt that youngsters these days didn't appear to know very much about the Holocaust.

Jack told him about the plight of the Goldbergs. And he told him how Myra had behaved throughout their married life, and how he had tried to help her, treating her better than she deserved. He made it clear that any money José felt he had a claim to would come from Myra's estate, even though he had given the money to her. He also explained about the villa in Spain, wondering if this was the connection with José, which he felt sure it was.

Indeed, his thoughts bore fruit. José explained that his father, Antonio, was seduced by Myra, when she was staying at the villa. It was a shortlived affair, but Myra had become pregnant with Antonio's son, José. He explained that Myra was all set to have an abortion, but Antonio persuaded her that with Franco in power in Spain at that time, she could find herself in deeper trouble. So, she gave birth.

The baby was taken away by the authorities, and Antonio and Myra were told that it had died. Tragically, such things happened in Franco's Spain; the practice became known as "niños robados": stolen children. It was a terrible scandal, and would not be completely exposed for some time to come. Under Franco's dictatorship, it was commonly deemed appropriate to take children from "undesirable" parents and sell them to "approved" families. The fact that priests and nuns did this was appalling.

Myra couldn't care less, and happily accepted that the baby had died; what a relief! She could return to Britain and no one would even know about it. Antonio was disgusted with her.

He had never truly believed that his baby had died; he and Myra were both fit and healthy. He had heard rumours of other parents who were also suspicious of these "deaths", and spent a lifetime searching for the truth.

After years of searching, Antonio managed to force a nun in the nearby hospital to show him the records of births and deaths. There was indeed a record of birth by a certain Myra Blake, an "undesirable" from Britain, who had given birth in 1947. There was also a false record of death; in truth, the baby had been given to an "approved" family in Barcelona. With the help of the nun, Antonio was able to trace the whereabouts of his son. The Sanchez family had moved several times, so it took years of searching, until he finally found his son just two years ago, in 1964.

When José realized that the people he had been living with were not his real family, he was devastated. They told him that he had been given to them by a priest, and were assured that they were giving a good home to the child of undesirables – all they had to do was make a donation to the Church.

José was very angry; he felt like a pet bought in a store. He left the only home he had ever known and returned to Santiago de la Ribera, to live with Antonio, his real father.

Antonio told him all about Myra, and how the nuns had told them that their baby had died. He told José all about his real family, his grandmother Maria and how he had set himself up in business.

Last year a news report came on the television, explaining that the wife of multi-millionaire Jack Blake, founder of the Blake Charity Foundation for homeless people, had died. Antonio and José saw photographs of her in the newspapers and, with the unusual name Myra, felt sure that she was the one. They carried out their investigations and decided to trace José's roots.

"So, you see, Señor Blake, I was and still am full of anger at the way I have been treated – not only by the Spanish authorities, and the family who lied to me, but by Myra, my real mother."

"Please call me Jack, José. We are all victims of Myra's mental health problems. I tried for years to make her see sense and get help, but she was a dual personality; she could be a wonderful mother to Andrew, then happily ditch you. She only married me because of the fortune I inherited, and became angry when I set up this charity, even though I had already made her a millionaire."

"Oh, Jack, I'm so sorry; I had no idea. My father and I didn't know what to expect. We're not after money, though I know I mentioned that on the phone to you, when I was angry. I just wanted to know the truth about my origins."

"How did you know we had relatives in Berlin? And where did you get the idea that it was Nazi gold?"

"The newspaper reports went into great detail about your family; one newspaper mentioned that your father was married to a German. The charity is famous, and seen as a model in Europe, so when Myra died it made the headlines – even in Spain. When I knew there was a German connection, I just made up the Nazi gold thing to get your attention." José looked down, apologetically.

"José, it's time you met Andrew, your half-brother, and other members of the family. Where are you staying?"

"I'm at a hotel in central London."

"Well, you must stay with me while we sort this all out. I insist."

"I don't want to be any trouble, Jack, really. And I can't leave my father for too long; since my grandmother died, he's on his own. Although he's now found me, years of searching have taken their toll."

"You'll be no trouble at all. Settle up with the hotel and come back here with your suitcase; I'll take you to my house and get you settled in. Take the tube. Are you familiar with the Underground?"

"Yes, I love it! We have it in Madrid, but not in any of the other cities near where we live."

"Good. I'll see you later, then."

José went back to the hotel and made a phone call to his father, to tell him that things were working out well, and that he mustn't worry; Jack was very sympathetic and wanted to put things right. Then, he checked out and made his way back to Jack's office.

Chapter 9

1947

SANTIAGO DE LA RIBERA, SPAIN

"HI, GORGEOUS. SUNBATHING again?"

Myra had crossed the road from the villa when she saw Antonio quickly walking past. He had tried not to look at the villa, but curiosity got the better of him – unfortunately Myra was coming out and crossing the road, just as he was passing by. He saw her sigh.

"Myra, why did you lie to me, that you would be back in a month's time?"

"Oh, I'm a free spirit, darling; I do things on the spur of the moment. Talking of which, I've got some news for you: I'm pregnant, and the baby has to be yours."

Antonio froze and looked at her. For a while he was speechless.

"Well? Say something."

"I don't know what to say," he gasped. "How can you be sure it's mine? We were only together a short time, before you returned to Britain."

"Oh, it's yours, alright; Jack and I haven't had sex since my son Andrew was born."

"You're married… with a child?"

"Yes, sweetheart. Didn't I tell you?"

He looked at her in silence.

"I've come here to have an abortion, before it starts to show."

"That cannot happen; it's not as easy as you think. We need to talk about this."

"Well, come inside the villa, and we'll have a chat and work things out."

Myra led the way, and reluctantly Antonio entered the villa. He stayed in the lounge, while Myra went to make coffee. Immediately once she had returned from the kitchen, she started to make plans.

"You're going to help me get this done before I return home. You must know a doctor or nurse who will do this."

"No, I don't; you are very much mistaken. We are not a democracy here; government is in the strong grip of General Franco and the Church. If the authorities found out you had an abortion, you could be in serious trouble and put in prison. I could be jailed, too, for helping you."

"How primitive!"

"You're going to have to have the baby here. You'll need to inform your family, and they will have to come out, so we can discuss the way forward, sensibly. I will take responsibility and help with the child."

"In your dreams, sweetheart!"

"Be sensible, Myra, for goodness' sake. I'll make an appointment with our doctor and we'll take it from there."

"I can't stay here until the baby is born! I can't leave Andrew for that amount of time!"

"How far gone are you?"

"About twenty-three weeks."

"I don't know much about these things, but an abortion at this stage sounds dangerous, anyway! I'll go and make an appointment right now, and come back later to let you know." Antonio left, abruptly.

He was stunned. He had to make sure this didn't hamper his plans for the future. He didn't know what his mother would make of it all; he would have to conceal it from her, somehow.

He went to the medical centre, explained things without revealing too much, and was lucky to get an appointment for the following morning.

Myra would have to say that she was ill or something, and that she couldn't return to Britain for a while. No, that wouldn't work: her family would want to come out and visit her and, if possible, make arrangements to take her home. What on Earth were they going to do?!

He went straight back to the villa to prepare Myra for the following morning.

"Hi, sweetheart, how did you get on?" she asked.

"Please stop calling me that. My name is Antonio and I'm

certainly not your sweetheart! If I was, then you wouldn't treat me the way you have! We have an appointment for tomorrow morning at eight-thirty."

"Bloody hell, love – that's early for me!"

"Well, if you want my help, you'll be ready. And, you'll have to come clean with your family and tell them."

"I can't; the authorities in Britain are nearly as primitive as they are here. They might take Andrew away from me and put him in care."

"That might be the best thing that could happen to him! What about your husband?"

"We split up."

"What a mess! What are we going to do?"

They talked through several options.

In the end, Myra said that she would go home. The baby wasn't showing yet anyway, and she would be careful to conceal the bump with tight-fitting clothes, until it became too difficult. Then, she would make one of her customary visits to Spain, where she would declare that she was feeling a little unwell, and would need to stay longer than usual. Then, hopefully the baby would come on time, or even early, and she could return to Britain.

She told him to make arrangements for the baby to go to an orphanage, but Antonio knew deep down that he would never let that happen; he was going to come clean with his mother, and they would bring the baby up without Myra. He knew that his mother would come around in the end, and would indeed be delighted with a grandchild. She had been widowed young.

Antonio had never known his father, who worked for a distribution company which supplied peppers, artichokes, potatoes and other vegetables to local retailers. He was hoping soon to have his own business, and that would make things a lot easier with the child. Myra need never know.

"You'll make sure that the baby goes to a nice orphanage, won't you; some nice nuns somewhere will do a good job, I'm sure."

"Just leave all that to me."

Myra made arrangements to return home. She was a little apprehensive about the timescale of things, and unhappy that she couldn't just get rid of the baby, but she was confident that Antonio was a decent man and would do the right thing. She briefly even considered divorcing Jack and making a new life in Spain, with Andrew, Antonio and the new baby, but she knew that it wouldn't last; she would grow fed up with being tied down, and knew that it would only be a matter of time before she would want to move on. It would be more difficult in a foreign country, especially with this tyrant Franco in power, and she would be trapped. *Better to move on now,* she thought.

Chapter 10

1945

AUSCHWITZ, POLAND

AARON STARED AT the pile of corpses and wondered if his mother, sister or father were amongst them.

His wonderful mother, who was so dignified, such a lady, so elegant... Everyone looked up to her. She was a striking woman, and was very well loved and respected in the community. She would often invite neighbours and friends who were not very well off, and treat them to a splendid dinner party. She worked voluntarily for a charity, to help those less fortunate than herself. Of course, none of this mattered to the fascist Nazi thugs.

His beautiful sister, who was so talented; she could play the piano with her eyes closed. The family had great hopes that she would become a concert pianist – in fact, her piano tutor said it was almost a given. She had a very bright future ahead of her. When their mother had the friends and neighbours in, Rachel would play and thrill them.

His father, so skilled at making jewellery… He had inherited the business from his own father, and his father before him. Rueben employed many people in the workshop and jewellery store, and passed his knowledge and expertise on to them. He was loved and respected by his employees, and he treated them very well. Many wealthy and important people bought their jewellery from him; there was a huge market for his goods. Rueben was a tall, strong and very handsome man, who caught the eye of many of the ladies in the community.

That had all been stolen by these moronic thugs who claimed to be the "Master Race".

Aaron felt the whip land on his back, and he shuddered out of his daydreaming.

"Keep digging, Jew, or you'll join that pile of shit sooner than later."

Aaron got back to digging the trench with the other prisoners. He knew that, when the trench was dug, they would have to throw the bodies in and cover them over. He wondered why they were having to do this; had the crematoria broken down? He also knew that, after they had dug deep enough to throw the bodies into the pit, he and his fellow diggers would be shot and thrown in after them. He calculated that, at the rate they were digging, it would be about two more days before they were throwing the bodies in… and then their fate would be sealed. He had to find a way to join another work crew before then.

He didn't have to worry for long, though; things were changing…

"Jüdische schweine, bewegen!" *(Move, Jewish pigs!)* barked the S.S. officer. "We're moving you to another camp."

Aaron was anguished. Rumours were abundant that the Allies were very near and the Germans were destroying the crematoria, desperate to conceal what had happened here. Now he knew why they had been digging trenches and burying the corpses.

And now they were being moved to another camp! Why, oh, why, could they not just let them go?! The war was nearly over! Yet, the twisted Nazi mind still determined to eliminate as many Jews as possible, before the final defeat of Germany. There were even rumours that they had been throwing living children into the ovens, in their haste to destroy the Jewish race.

On January 18th, 1945, the Germans started to evacuate the prisoners of Auschwitz; they were marched to Wodzisla.

The journey to Wodzisla was horrendous. It was January, freezing cold and thick with snow, and the prisoners had to walk. Many died on the way. If they fell, they were shot, just in case they were faking it; the Nazis didn't want to leave any living witnesses. Aaron prayed, to a god he had lost faith in, that he would make it.

After a long, hellish journey, they eventually reached Wodzisla, where they were placed on crowded freight trains and shipped to other concentration camps, farther west. The train journey from there was another hell, reminding him of the long journey from Berlin to Auschwitz.

Finally, they found themselves at Gross-Rosen concentration camp.

This camp was already overcrowded before Aaron and the thousands of other pathetic victims made it to the gates. They were forced inside and found themselves just… there. The excuse for accommodation was already full; there was no food for them, and no blankets for warmth, to sleep at night; they melted snow for water. Huddled together in the snow, with fellow victims, sleep did not come easily. Many died in the night; Aaron often woke up to find the person huddled next to him a corpse.

They were surprised to find that they were not put to work; the Germans seemed preoccupied. Then, one day, they saw them loading trucks and driving off in a hurry. The prisoners were bewildered and prayed that they would be liberated.

They dared to search the barns and huts, but found very little to eat or comfort themselves with. Some of them tried to break open the gates, but the guards had left the electric fencing switched on; it wasn't possible.

Then, on 13th February, 1945, they heard trucks. They feared that the Germans had returned.

But it was the Soviets. They had come to liberate the camp.

It was no wonder that the Germans had fled: there was no mercy for Germans after the way they had treated the Russians, when the Nazis invaded and occupied their homeland.

Aaron felt elated, thanking God that he had made it. He dreamt of returning home, of making a new life. He knew that his wonderful family had been murdered, but he was determined to restore the family fortune, to make a new life and to honour the memory of his mother, father and sister. He joined the others in embracing the soldiers, and taking food and comfort. It was a slow process; they had been warned not to eat too much, or they might have greater problems. Little and often proved to be the healing process.

After some months, Aaron was moved to a transit camp. There he continued to recover slowly and, some months later, after a medical examination, he was deemed fit enough to travel.

Like everyone else, he was given a *Certificate of Liberation*, which allowed him to travel.

He was determined to make his way back to Berlin and reclaim the family home.

Chapter 11

1966

LONDON

JACK PHONED ANDREW.

"Andrew, José has been to see me. We need to set up a meeting with him, Uncle Joe and Auntie Clare."

"Oh, how did it go?"

"Too complicated to explain over the phone, son. You will not believe your ears; I think it will all come better from José. He's a nice lad; you couldn't wish for a better half-brother."

"Oh, okay. Where shall we meet?"

"Well, I think this office will be neutral ground. I'll get in touch with Joe and Clare and let you know."

Andrew put the phone down and couldn't help feeling apprehensive about meeting José, his half-brother! How would things work out? Everything had been like a whirlwind lately: first meeting his father and forming a new relationship with him, then learning all about his mother, and now this! Where would it all lead to?

Jack rang Joe and Clare, and they arranged a meeting at the Blake Charity Foundation for the following day.

They waited patiently in Jack's office: Joe, Clare, Andrew and Jack. They were all anxious, to say the least.

While they waited, they discussed the fact that José had explained he and his father were not after money, but the legality of the situation meant that he was entitled to half of Myra's estate, at the time of her death. They agreed that the family solicitor could deal with this, and that the money was not a problem. Jack assured them all that, after hearing José's story, they would only be too eager to help. He hadn't told them anything yet, wanting José to be the one to tell his heartbreaking story.

At last, the buzzer sounded:

Bzzzzzzz!

"Hello, Josie. Please send José in."

She led José into the office, and went off to organize coffee and cakes. He made straight for Andrew.

"Hello, Andrew, I'm José. I'm sorry if I'm causing you and your family complications or problems, but I am probably as bewildered and confused as you all are, and I need you to listen to my story."

"That's fine, José. That's why we're all here. Take your time." It felt so strange, like looking at a male version of his mother. There could be no doubt they were brothers.

Andrew introduced José to his aunt and uncle. José shook hands with everyone, and mentioned that his father had met Joe and Clare at the villa in Spain. Joe was taken aback by the first realization that this was indeed a genuine situation, together with the fact that José was his nephew – a male, Spanish replica of Myra.

After introductions, they made themselves comfortable in the seating area near the window, on plush sofas with a fabulous view of the city. Josie came in with a tray of coffee and cakes, and left them to it.

"Well, José, just tell them your story, as you told it to me the other day."

José began, leaving out none of the details. As he continued with his heartbreaking story, the faces of Andrew, Joe and Clare changed to ashen in colour, accompanied by gasps and moans. He told them of Myra's affair with his father Antonio, and of her dumping him, then her sudden return to Spain to announce her pregnancy, her desire for abortion, the scandal of the "niños rebados" and all that involved. He told them of his father's search for him and of their reunion. He expressed his feelings at how his childhood had been hijacked, and the new life he was now having to make.

Silence…

"As I said to you, José," Jack croaked, "we are all victims here of Myra's mental health problems."

"Absolutely," said Andrew. "Welcome to the family!"

"I think we need to speak to our family solicitor and make

amends somehow. What do you all think?"

"I'm not after money," said José.

"I know that but, after the way you have been treated, I don't think any of us would be happy unless we do this," said Andrew.

They all agreed, and Jack immediately phoned their solicitor to set up a meeting.

José said that he wouldn't attend, and would be happy with whatever arrangement they came up with; he already had a good job in his father's business. As a young man, Antonio had started working for a fruit and vegetable distribution firm, then eventually had set himself up in his own business, which was now flourishing, with the growth of tourism in the area. He wasn't short of money. Still, the others all agreed that it was a matter of principle.

"When all this is settled, we must come out to Spain and stay at the villa. It will be good to meet up with your father and for us all to get better acquainted," said Jack.

Andrew said: "Great, I can't wait! But first I have to go to Berlin; I need to find out what happened to the Goldbergs. I mean, I can guess it was Auschwitz, or some other hellhole devised by the golden-haired, blue-eyed 'Master Race', but my conscience is pricking me."

They spent some time filling in José on some family history, and Andrew's recent enlightenment about his— *their* mother. José, in turn, told them all about his old life in Barcelona, and his new life with his long-lost father. They were all fascinated with his description of Spain under Franco's domination.

When they were ready to leave, José returned to his hotel, where he rang his father again, to give him an update.

"Hola, Papá! It's me, José. I think everything will be okay. They did not reject me; the whole family believed my story, and have great sympathy with what I have been through… and what you have been through, of course."

"That's great, my son, that's great! We now have a family, of sorts. They must all come out and stay at the villa, and we can get to know each other better. When are you coming home?"

"I'm looking at flights soon, and hope to be home before the weekend, so I can be back at work on Monday."

"Don't worry about that; Julio is doing a fine job managing everything for me."

"My uncle, Joe, wishes to be remembered to you; he's looking forward to meeting you again. He remembers you turning up at the villa one day, asking for Myra."

"Well, well, I remember it, too! At least they know now that we're not making any of this up. Hopefully, the success of our business will also convince them that we're not after money."

"I told them that, but they insist that I should have something of Myra's estate. Actually, I don't want anything from a woman who was initially prepared to have me aborted, and was happy for me to be taken away, presumed dead!"

"I know, José. I know how hard this has all been for you, but we must all look to the future now and make a new life. Only good can come from this now, I feel. We have a new family."

"Yes, Papá, you're right."

Chapter 12

1966

BERLIN

ANDREW FLEW TO Berlin. He was amazed at how beautiful the city was; huge reconstruction works had rebuilt it to a wonderful standard. The only downside was that it was blighted by being divided.

The western sector was splendid, enjoying all the decencies of modern western civilization. Not so the eastern sector! Here, the cold, severe, heartless, godless mentality of communism prevailed. He remembered someone on the plane commenting that communism was "all things in poverty", rather than all things in common. With the use of binoculars, he could see from his hotel room over the wall to the eastern sector, and make out the grim, concrete constructions which housed the population. They looked like prison blocks.

He settled into his hotel and enjoyed a wonderful lunch. Then, he did some sightseeing and phoned home to tell his father that he had arrived safely.

The next day, with help from the British consulate, he made his way to the Berlin Jewish Museum. Here, he learned much about the fate of Jews in the Nazi period, throughout the whole of the Third Reich and particularly in Berlin. He already knew a bit about it, but was horrified at the more detailed facts he learnt. It wasn't presently taught in schools, and he wondered why not. However, the information he was given wasn't really specific enough.

He was questioned by the staff about his motives for requiring the information, and briefly explained his mission. He was then directed to the Berlin Restitutional Offices – but first he needed a brandy to help digest the horrors he had learnt about in the museum. How could intelligent people do this to other human beings? It frightened him, and made him realize that everything must be done to ensure that it never happened again. After a coffee and brandy in a delightful coffee house, he made his way to the Restitutional Offices.

Once there, he realized that this might be a long job. However, the staff were very helpful, though once again wanted to know his motives. Without mentioning the family fortune, he explained that his grandmother was Jewish and had relatives in Berlin at the time of the Nazi persecution; he wanted to know if there were any living relatives. He had a copy of his grandfather's wedding certificate, which displayed his grandmother's maiden name as Rebecca Goldberg. It was a huge advantage having this information and knowing the name Goldberg.

Astonishingly, due to a remarkably efficient filing system, in no time at all records were found for the Goldbergs. Indeed, they had owned a jewellery business and workshop in central Berlin. The names of the family were Rueben and Esther – husband and wife – and the children, Aaron and Rachel. There had also been grandparents, Moses and Hannah, but they had both died before the troubles began. There was also another: Rebecca, a sister of Hannah, but she had moved to England and married an Englishman by the name of Harold Blake, many years ago. Andrew was stunned; everything the bank manager had told them was true.

The records showed that the whole family had been deported to Auschwitz, but there were no further entries. Andrew asked if there had been any survivors, and how he might make further investigations. The clerk looked at him and said that this would be very difficult: the area of Berlin in which they lived was now within the eastern sector; if anyone had survived, they would have probably made their way there, not knowing the political situation, and found themselves trapped in the communist block.

Still, the clerk explained that, although it might be difficult, a visa could be obtained for a few hours' visit to the eastern sector. He gave Andrew the address the Goldbergs had lived at, making sure he understood that it may have been totally destroyed and a new set of buildings constructed. He also gave him the address of the office where he needed to obtain the visa – if it was at all possible.

Andrew then called in to the British consulate and asked for some advice. He was shown into an office where a young man listened to his story, and his question of whether or not it was dangerous to enter the eastern side. The young man said that, if he were able to get a visa, then it might be possible for someone from the consulate to go with him.

"Oh, that would be so helpful. I'm a little bit nervous about going there on my own."

"No problem. I'll see if I can be the one to accompany you; I'm rather sympathetic to your story."

"That would be good. What's your name?"

"It's John."

"Thank you, John. Thanks so much for your help."

Andrew went back to his hotel, thoroughly depressed, and ordered a large brandy. He ventured into the dining room and ordered his evening meal, after which he rang his father and gave him an update. Jack was pleased that the story matched what they had already been told, but was very worried about Andrew entering the eastern sector.

"I'll be okay, Dad; I won't go without an official visa, and somebody from the consulate will be coming with me."

"Well, let's hope so. Be careful, please."

The next day, he went to the Central Bureau and made an application for a visa. He was thoroughly questioned, but he told the truth – leaving out the bit about the family fortune. It seemed genuine enough, given the copies of the documents he had with him from the Restitutional Office, and he was granted a visa, which was valid for eight hours. He was advised to go early in the morning, so as not to be returning too late. It had been known for some people not to return after a certain time of the evening.

Back at the hotel he ate lunch, enjoyed some more sightseeing in the city and had an early night, ready to be up in the morning for an early start.

The address he had been given was 13 Hans-Otto-Straffe – he wondered what he would find there.

In the morning, a porter rang his hotel room and told him that a person from the British consulate wanted to speak to him. It was John, confirming that he would be accompanying Andrew. He was delighted, and made his way to the consulate after breakfast.

John met him in the foyer, and together they caught a cab to the checkpoint. John knew exactly where to go, and all the right things to say; Andrew was so relieved.

They passed through several checkpoints, where the guards seemed to take delight in asking for papers, questioning the purpose of their visit and so on. Finally, they made it through.

Andrew was aghast at the grimness of the whole area. He had seen it at a distance, from his hotel room with binoculars, but to be here, standing on the other side of the wall, was something else. It felt eerie, cold, colourless and devoid of people; lifeless, almost. As they made their way through the streets, the place seemed to come alive a little bit, but people looked at them as if they were from another planet, in their stylish western clothes.

They made a few enquiries, while trying to follow an out-of-date map, and eventually found themselves on Hans-Otto-Straffe. Some parts of the street comprised "modern" concrete apartment blocks, while in others the original buildings seemed to have been restored.

Miraculously, number thirteen was in a section which seemed to be original; it was not an apartment, but a detached house. Looking at it, they could clearly see that it had been a very grand house at one time, with grounds all around it. Alas, though, when they approached the front door, they could see a cluster of doorbells; in true communist style there were now several families living in this large house. John suggested ringing number one. The house still had *"13"* chiselled into the stonework above the entrance, so perhaps the original owner might now be in the first apartment, of which there were six. So, Andrew rang the doorbell for number one.

Someone came to the main door: a thin, hard-looking woman who was poorly dressed; she looked at them with suspicion. "What do you want?"

John answered in impeccable German: "We were wondering if you might know if any of the original inhabitants of this premises still live here. Their names were Goldberg."

She looked at them even more suspiciously, then retorted: "The Nazis moved them out, over twenty years ago. There's nobody here now by that name."

"Is there anyone here who might know if one or more of the family survived the Holocaust, and where they might be now?"

"Try Herr Grüber in number three. He was the first to move in; he might know."

With that, the door slammed shut.

"She must be a true communist," said John.

Andrew rang the doorbell for number three. An elderly gentleman with a friendly face came to the main door.

"Hello, Herr Grüber. Your neighbour in number one told us that you might be able to help us locate the original family of Jews who lived here. Their name was Goldberg," Andrew said, pleasantly.

"Oh, yes, I remember the Goldbergs. They were lovely people – taken away by those filthy Nazis! Come in, come in. Hopefully I can tell you what you want to know."

Herr Grüber made them coffee and told them his story. He explained that he knew the family well, and could remember the day they were removed from their home. It was heartbreaking, he said.

"I can still see the anguished, bewildered faces, as they were brutally thrown into an overcrowded truck. My wife and I cried. We had known Hannah, Reuben's mother, before she died, and had got to know Esther after she had married Rueben. They were very kind and generous people; we were often invited to dinner parties, along with other neighbours."

Herr Grüber went on to explain how a family of Nazis then occupied the grand house. They were rude and arrogant, looking down on the neighbours. They were very suspicious that the neighbours had all been "Jew lovers", so all tried to keep out of their way. The young boy was in the Hitler Youth – an arrogant little thing – and the father was an S.S. officer, as heartless and brutal as the rest of them. The mother joined the Women's League. She, too, was cold and unfriendly.

The father died on the Russian front; the boy died trying to defend Berlin as the Allies approached. The mother, like many

German women, was repeatedly raped by Russian soldiers and left for dead. The victors showed no mercy after what the Germans had done to their homeland.

Aaron Goldberg had survived Auschwitz and returned to the house, only to find that the Soviets were turning it into the flats which now formed the old house. Aaron protested that he was the rightful owner but, after making a fuss, he was arrested and taken away. Nothing was heard about him since.

"Gosh," said Andrew, "he must still be alive!"

He turned to John: "Is there any way I can find out? You see, his great aunt was my grandmother, who moved to England before the Nazis and married my grandfather."

"Wow," said John, "you didn't mention that!"

"It's really only just dawning on me, to be honest. This whole thing has only recently come to light. Where can I make further enquiries?"

"I can try and do that for you, but it will take time. The Soviets are not very helpful, as you can imagine."

Herr Grüber was delighted to hear this. "Oh, if only you could locate him, then justice could be done and he could return to his home! What's left of it!"

They thanked Herr Grüber and made their way back to the western sector.

John told Andrew to return to Britain and wait for him to make enquiries. They exchanged telephone numbers and addresses, and bade each other farewell. Andrew telephoned his father with an update, then booked flights home.

Chapter 13

1945

POLAND

THE RED CROSS provided Aaron with medication, warm clothes, food, travel passes and money, together with his *Certificate of Liberation*. Then they directed him to a train which would take him to Berlin – a real train, not a cattle truck. He couldn't believe his good fortune; although still traumatized and scarred by all he had been through, and the horrors he had witnessed, together with the loss of his loved ones, he felt excited at returning home and reclaiming the family house.

The journey was long and the train was filled with people of all ages, who had been liberated from the camps and deemed well enough to travel. They did not speak to one another; everyone looked lifeless. It was as if the privilege of living had been beaten out of them.

They stopped at various stations, eventually reaching the border with eastern Germany. Here there was a horrendous delay, and Aaron thought they might be sent back. The Russian soldiers were determined to check everyone's papers, even though the guardsmen had assured them that this had been done thoroughly before leaving Poland. They were insistent, explaining that some Nazi guards had slipped through the net, taking prisoners' clothes and masquerading as victims. Aaron could hear these conversations and panicked; he wondered if the person sitting opposite him was such an imposter!

After what seemed an age, the soldiers were satisfied, and the train moved on into Germany. There were more stops on the way, and checking of papers, until at last they reached Berlin.

Weary with travel, Aaron stepped onto the platform. A chill ran down his spine, because the last time at this station he was on the siding with his beloved family and other Jews, before they were all herded into cattle trucks like animals. He could still hear the women and children screaming, the S.S. pigs barking and whipping them, and the dogs snarling viciously.

He sighed, pulled himself together and made his way to Hans-Otto-Straffe, excited to be home.

Alas, how could he not have realized that the Allied bombing would have destroyed the city? Everywhere he looked there was destruction and devastation; few buildings had survived. There were women picking up rubble and stones, clearing away the devastation.

One part of him thought: *Serves you right! This is what you get for following a lunatic!* However, he fully knew that normal German people had not followed the regime and had kept silent.

As he entered his street, he could see widespread destruction; most of the houses had been flattened, though some were still standing, but in very poor condition. One or two of the more substantial houses seemed to have fared better. He hoped that number 13 had been spared, or was at least reparable.

In the distance he could see the house. It had evidently been damaged, but there were workmen around it. *They must be repairing it,* he thought. As he approached, he could see that armed Russian soldiers were supervising a work gang of German men and women, as they repaired the damage. He approached one of the soldiers who seemed to be in charge, and explained that this was his house.

"Officer, I have been liberated from a concentration camp by your good soldiers, and have just returned to Berlin. This is my family home."

The Russian officer looked as sinister as any he had seen in Auschwitz. Was that angry menacing look deemed to be requisite for all soldiers of dictatorships?

"This house has been requisitioned by the State and is being turned into apartments," the soldier growled. "It is impossible for one person or even one family to live in such splendour; the U.S.S.R. does not permit such debauchery."

Aaron was stunned.

"It's my property! My father, mother, sister and I lived here, until the Nazis took us away and stole everything."

"You can't prove that, and even if you could nothing can be done now. The war has changed everything."

"But that's not fair!"

At that moment, Aaron noticed one of his old neighbours nearby. It was Herr Grüber, an old friend of the family.

"Herr Grüber! It's me, Aaron. You remember me?"

Herr Grüber stared for a moment… The thin, straggly, unkempt person speaking to him was unrecognizable. Yet, there was something…

"Aaron! Oh, Aaron, my boy, you're alive! You survived!"

"Yes, it's me."

They embraced.

Herr Grüber was moved to tears, as Aaron explained that his mother, father and sister had perished in Auschwitz.

"Those murdering bastards! This is their punishment," spat Herr Grüber, pointing to the work gang of former German soldiers rebuilding the house. They were thin, undernourished and wearing ragged clothes. *Still not as thin as some of their victims in the camps, though,* thought Aaron, bitterly.

"Herr Grüber, would you be so kind as to explain to the officer here that this is my home?"

"Why, of course, my boy, of course."

He turned to the Russian and explained that he had known the family for a very long time; Aaron was the rightful owner.

"You can't prove that!" said the officer.

"Well, actually, officer, yes I can most definitely prove it!" argued Herr Grüber. "Just follow me inside the house, please."

Aaron and the Russian officer followed him into the back of the house. Aaron was filled with emotion as he stepped into his old home. The family furniture had gone, replaced with different items, most of which were now damaged.

However, the old German dresser caught his eye; his mother and grandmother's pride and joy – it was still here! It was to this piece of furniture that Herr Grüber now led them.

"Behind this dresser is the evidence you need," he said.

Aaron was perplexed, as the Russian shouted something out of the window. Two soldiers came in from the street and were instructed to move the heavy piece of furniture. When they failed, another two soldiers came to assist.

When they had moved the dresser, Herr Grüber pointed to photographs, birth certificates, wedding certificates and a letter, all pasted to the back of the dresser. Aaron immediately recognized the family photos and eagerly pointed to himself – younger and fitter, but unmistakably him. His mother and father's wedding certificate, and the birth certificates of he and his sister, Rachel, were all authentic.

There was a letter:

"To whom it may concern.

The rightful owners of this property are Rueben and Esther Goldberg, and their two children Aaron and Rachel. We are in fear of being deported by the Nazis. If this should happen, then proof of ownership can be traced through our bank. If none of us should survive this persecution, then the rightful owner would be Rueben's aunt Elizabeth, who moved to England many years ago. The Reichsbank will have all of the details.

I hope that this evidence will survive, and that the Nazis won't find it and destroy it.

Rueben Goldberg."

Aaron burst into uncontrollable tears.

Herr Grüber held him fast and explained that, in his wisdom, Reuben could see all that was coming, and pasted all of this to the back of the dresser, in the hope that the new occupants would not be able to move it. It had worked.

The Russian officer took all of the photographs, certificates and the letter, and told Aaron to follow him. Aaron hugged Herr Grüber once more and thanked him, saying that he would see him later. But that was not going to happen…

Chapter 14

1966

LONDON

ANDREW LANDED SAFELY at Heathrow, and passed through customs with no problems. Jack met him at Arrivals, and they made their way to the car park. On the way home, Andrew gave him a full update on all that had happened.

"This Aaron Goldberg could still be alive somewhere, Dad. He's the rightful heir to everything!"

"Not everything, Andrew; there's the money my father already had before he inherited the Goldberg fortune, which he left to me. It's that money I used to buy the villa in Spain, so that can't be claimed by anyone. The money I gave to your mother has now been legally inherited by you, and with her death it should not be a problem. As far as the trust fund I set up for you goes, if we have to lose that you will still be financially sound from the interest it has made over all these years, and the investment in your business."

"Yes, but what if the authorities say that the interest should go to Aaron Goldberg, too? How on Earth are we going to work all this out?"

"Well, it will have to be done legally, and we will have to accept the outcome. It will be a pity if the charity suffers."

"Yes, I know, but my conscience will not allow me to ignore Aaron Goldberg, now that we know there's a possibility that he is still alive. I'm going to have to find him, Dad."

"Yes, Andrew, we'll do that. Let's wait and see what the British consulate in Berlin comes up with."

Andrew returned to his apartment in Knightsbridge and unpacked. Then, he spent the rest of the day catching up on the business, and found everything to be in order. He had a good staff – reliable and hardworking – and all was well.

He sat down and did some sums. If his father was right, then, taking away his mother's million and the money in the trust fund, then given the value of his business – which he could only guess at – he would be worth about a million, plus his apartment and the boutique. However, if the legal system declared that any interest, be it monetary or in property, should be seen as part of that original inheritance, then he would be doomed, and so would his father! His father had only bought a house out of the money, and given some to Myra and Uncle Joe; most had been invested in the charity. And then there was José! What about his claims!?

Oh, well, he thought to himself, with humour, *we'll all have to live in the villa in Spain and get jobs out there.*

In seriousness, Franco had declared that tourism was the way forward, and there were resorts being built everywhere. From the villa in Santiago de la Ribera, one could see high-rise hotels being built on the Manga Strip. This would take years to develop, but it could be the way forward.

He rang his father, and they arranged to meet up with Joe, Clare and José the following day. Then, he opened a bottle of Scotch and sat down, pondering everything. What a turn his life had taken in so short a time: his mother's death; finding out about her problems; reuniting with his father; learning all about the family fortune, the Goldbergs, a half-brother, Aaron…!

"Where are you, Aaron?" he said out loud. After all that his family had endured, Andrew was determined to find him.

The next day, they all met up at Joe and Clare's house. Andrew gave a detailed account of everything he had learnt from his visit to Berlin.

They sat in silence, stunned to hear the tragic story of the Goldberg family. Clare shed tears. Joe immediately said: "We must find him – if he's alive, that is. Right must be done! Those filthy Nazis!"

Jack looked bewildered and said: "I cannot understand why my father never spoke about this. I know that my mother died before any of these troubles started, but surely my father could have spoken to me, and told me about my mother's relations in Berlin. He could have told me all about my grandmother's life in Germany before she met him. It was rarely mentioned; the only thing which ever reminded me about the situation was the Christmas cards from Germany. These ceased, of course, when that slimy maniac took power."

"Your father might have known, Jack, but felt it ought to be kept unspoken about. They were terrible times. He only had a lucky escape in the Blitz, remember. Then later the dementia started to set in," reasoned Joe.

José, who had been silent through all of this, then declared: "I want to help find this Aaron. I know what it's like to be rejected and not have a family. I'll help you, Andrew."

"That's great, José. I'm waiting to hear from a Mr. John Sullivan at the British consulate in Berlin. Earlier I told you that he was kind enough to escort me to the eastern sector in Berlin, and now he's following up Herr Grüber's story, to see if he can trace Aaron. Once we have a lead, then I guess it's off to Berlin, José."

"Dad, a letter has come this morning, from Berlin."

"Gosh, that was quick work! What does it say?"

"John Sullivan says that after the Russian officer took the photographs, documents and letter off the back of the German dresser, he and Aaron went to the local military police depot. There, he was interrogated and classed as a spy. He was sent off to Siberia, to work in some labour camp, as a political prisoner."

"Oh, my god! After what that poor boy had been through, to then be treated like that is criminal!"

"I know! John says we should contact the Russian embassy here. He suggests taking evidence of Aaron's lost inheritance."

"The bank can help us there; Mr. Stanhope can provide us with all the evidence we need to take to the embassy. I'll ring him straight away."

"I'll give José an update. With all of these comings and goings and meetings, he might as well stay here with me; I have two spare rooms in this apartment."

"Yes, if that's okay with you, then it would make things easier.

Ask him; see what he says. He's wasting money staying at that hotel."

Andrew rang José, who was a little reluctant to accept, not wishing to impose. In the end he agreed, but said that he would first need to make a quick visit to Spain, for a day or two, to catch up with his father, and give him an update of all that was going on.

Meanwhile, Jack rang the bank in Manchester and spoke to George Stanhope, the deputy manager. George listened carefully, astounded to hear the fate of Aaron Goldberg.

"Let me think a moment..." he said. "Can I put you on hold, while I fish out the file again?"

"Yes, of course."

Soon, George came back on the line and said: "I think there's enough documentation here to convince the Russian embassy; it all depends how cooperative they are. It's this 'Cold War' thing, you know."

"Yes, I know."

"Listen, I'll come with you; we can meet up when I arrive from Manchester and go together. No disrespect, but it might come better from a bank official than someone else."

"Are you sure?"

"Absolutely. I feel partly involved in all this, having dealt with the case when your father died."

"Okay. That's very good of you."

"I'll ring the embassy and make an appointment."

They exchanged days and times which would be convenient and rang off.

Chapter 15

1947

SANTIAGO DE LA RIBERA, SPAIN

MYRA RETURNED TO the villa. Her pregnancy was advanced, and she couldn't wait to remove the tight-fitting corset she was wearing. At last, she felt relief and went looking for Antonio.

She knew his address, but wasn't sure if he would be in work or not; this siesta thing was a bit weird! However, she made her way there and found the house. It was a small bungalow type, with a front patio, in one of the side streets of San Javier. She knocked on the door and a very smart Spanish lady came to the door. Myra guessed it was his mother; she could quickly see where he got his good looks from.

"Oh, hello, I'm looking for Antonio."

In perfect English, the Spanish woman replied: "I'm sorry, but he's at work. I'm his mother. How can I help?"

Myra explained that she had met Antonio on one of her visits to Santiago, and just wanted to catch up.

His mother scrutinized her, taking note of her pregnant state. Who was this girl? How did Antonio know a pregnant British woman? Surely she should be in England; it looked as if the baby was due any day!

"Will you tell him that Myra called? He knows where to find me."

"Yes, of course. I'll tell him when he comes home for siesta."

Myra thanked her politely and turned to walk away. Maria looked after her and pondered.

It was a warm, sunny day, and Myra enjoyed the walk back to the villa. Once there, she poured a gin and tonic, and waited patiently for Antonio to come.

When Antonio arrived home, his mother looked at him, quizzically.

"You've had a visitor."

Antonio's stomach lurched. He had a feeling he knew what was coming.

"She said her name was Myra and that you'd know where to find her. She was heavily pregnant."

Silence…

"Antonio, how do you know a young, pregnant English woman?"

"She's just someone I met when I was at the beach last year. She's probably here for her annual holiday, and wanted to catch up."

"She looks as if the baby is due any day! Is there something you're not telling me?"

Again, silence…

"I guess your silence is explanation enough!"

"I'm sorry, Mama; I gave in to temptation! She seduced me, and the next time she came to Spain she told me she was pregnant! I was trapped!"

"I can see how easy it was to seduce you, Antonio; she's very beautiful."

Antonio told her everything; there was no point in lying. She would suspect odd behaviour as he went back and forth to the hospital, anyway.

"Why did you have to go to the house?" demanded Antonio. "You knew very well that I would be at work! I wanted to tell my mother myself, in my own way, privately, but you had to confront her, didn't you?!"

"Oh, come on, sweetheart, she'd have to know sooner or later!"

"Don't call me that; I'm not your sweetheart!"

"Well, I need to see a doctor and get myself sorted. I have healthcare in Britain which covers me here. So, where do we go?"

"We'll go to the surgery I took you to last time; they will advise us. There's a local hospital; you will probably be sent there."

"Oh, a sunny seaside birth. How nice."

"Start taking this seriously, please. We're talking about a life here: our baby!"

They went to the surgery the next morning, and were advised to register at the local hospital. So, they made their way there.

After some lengthy procedures, document signing and questioning – which is the Spanish way – she was finally registered. Then there were more lengthy procedures, including blood tests, blood pressure, etc., etc., etc…., before they could leave.

When they eventually returned to the villa, Antonio made some coffee and they discussed things further.

After a short while, Antonio left and went to the nearest bar on the seafront, for a Menu del Dia. He left her at the villa and gave her his phone number. Then he returned home and gave his mother an update.

"She shouldn't be on her own there," his mother offered; "she ought to stay here with us, Antonio."

"You won't like her, Mama: she may be beautiful, but it turns out she's not a very nice person to know."

"All the same, she's carrying your child; my grandchild!"

When Antonio went off to work – late – his mother rang the villa in Santiago de la Ribera.

"Hello, this is Maria, Antonio's mother, speaking. I do feel a little bit concerned that you are all alone there, in your condition. I was wondering if you would like to stay here with us, until the baby is born?"

"Oh, how sweet! That's very kind of you, but I couldn't impose on you like that. I think the baby is due any day now – the sooner the better, so that I can get back to England."

After a long silence, Maria said, coldly: "As you wish. But you have our telephone number. We can be with you in minutes from here in San Javier."

"Thank you, Maria. I have the number safe."

Maria hung up, still stunned at Myra's comments.

Antonio came back from work late that evening, having worked on, to make up for being late returning from siesta.

Maria immediately wanted to know everything.

He explained that Myra had originally wanted an abortion, but he had persuaded her that this was wrong. She made him promise to put the child in an orphanage.

"What kind of a woman is she? Doesn't she want to have any contact with her child?"

"I'm afraid not, Mama. I told you she's not a very nice person."

He explained that she was married with a baby, and that the authorities in England would probably take that baby away from her if they knew about all of this. She was also estranged from her husband. It was all an unsavoury mess.

Maria was shocked. But she said there was no way his child would be put into an orphanage; they would look after it together. She could work around that very well, as her English classes in the school were only part-time.

While the idea of a grandchild was delightful, they would have to tell the neighbours that it was a relative's child they were bringing up; Franco's regime was strict and in cahoots with the Church. Antonio's situation would be frowned upon; he could even lose his job!

"Not a word of this to Father Juan in church on Sunday, remember. We'll make up a story to cover ourselves."

Two days later, Myra telephoned Maria…

"My waters have broken! Help, I need to get to the hospital!"

"I'm on my way."

It took Maria very little time to get to the seafront, pick up Myra and take her to the hospital, which was just along the coastline. There, she was taken straight to the maternity ward and made comfortable by the nuns, who were nurses.

Maria asked if she could use the telephone to call her son, who was the father. She was shown into an office and quickly telephoned Antonio's place of work. She spoke to his boss, lying that she was unwell, and needed him to take her to the hospital. She dared not tell the man the truth; no one could know about this child, who was to be born out of wedlock. The only people from whom they couldn't hide the truth was the doctor and nurses; the documentation spoke for itself.

Antonio was there very quickly, and they waited patiently for news of the birth.

After what seemed an age, a nun came out with a graveyard face, and told them the child had died.

The hospital would deal with the body. As soon as the mother was fit enough to be moved, they could take her home.

Maria and Antonio were stunned.

"Surely this can't be right! Myra is in perfect health!"

"It happens that way sometimes, señor. We have no control over nature."

"I need to see the baby!"

"Hospital regulations do not allow that, as it is deemed too upsetting for the parents. As soon as your... wife... is well enough, you must take her home and care for her."

"I need to see her now."

"Yes, of course. Follow me."

Antonio and his mother followed the nun to Myra's bed.

"Oh, poor little mite! I think it was a boy," said Myra. "Anyway, problem solved, Antonio: I can return to England and you need have no worries now. What a relief! I need to book flights as soon as I can, before anyone at home suspects anything."

Antonio and Maria were speechless. They were glad the nun couldn't speak English, to understand Myra's heartless comments.

They said that they would call the next day, to see how Myra was. The nun replied that the hospital would contact them when she was well enough to be moved. Maria was quietly grateful for that: she couldn't quite cope with the thought of having to be nursemaid to this callous girl. The sooner she was on her way back to England, the better.

Antonio couldn't sleep that night; he felt that something was just not right. Was the baby deformed in some way, and the authorities were being kind, not allowing them to see it? Had she perhaps not been pregnant after all, and persuaded the nuns to keep her secret? Perhaps she had faked the whole thing, to get money out of him. No, that couldn't be possible; she was loaded! Just look at the villa!

After a sleepless night, he went to work and pondered what to do. He couldn't speak to his boss, for fear of losing his job, having had a child out of wedlock.

He returned home feeling despondent.

"Mama, I feel that something is wrong. It doesn't make sense that we couldn't see the baby. I know that Myra couldn't care less, and just wants to return to England, but I feel there's something not right here. Perhaps we should demand to see the baby."

"I think you're right, Antonio. I've been pondering this all day."

"I have spoken to my brother-in-law, Andres – Auntie Sonia's husband. He is a magistrate, as you know. He is sworn to secrecy, and was very helpful. He said that he has had several clients coming to seek his help with the same problem – all of them are convinced that something illegal is going on. He said that he and a few other magistrates are looking into the matter, but they have to be very careful, because of the Church and Franco."

"Wow! Do you think they have stolen the baby?"

"Something like that. But you know what Franco's regime is like: we are not a democracy; Andres will have to work with his friends in absolute secrecy."

As soon as she felt able to travel, Myra returned to England.

Once unpacked, she rang her brother to ask him and Clare to drop Andrew off. About an hour later they called, and she swooped Andrew up in her arms, smothering him with kisses and cuddles.

"Did you miss Mummy, darling?"

"Yes, Mummy, I did. Are you better now? We thought you would have been home sooner, but Uncle Joe said you were unwell."

"Yes, just a tummy bug, I think. But all is well; I'm here now."

But she didn't feel well at all; the stress of giving birth and travelling so soon afterward was taking its toll.

She thanked Joe and Clare for looking after Andrew, and handed them gifts in gratitude. Then, after they had gone, she felt she needed to get to bed early, so she opened the presents she had bought for Andrew. After he had exhausted himself enjoying his new toys, she made an early supper and put him to bed. Then, she poured herself a gin and tonic and made her way to bed, too.

Chapter 16

1966

LONDON

JACK LEFT THE tube station and entered Kensington Palace Gardens. Outside the station, George Stanhope was waiting for him, as arranged. They greeted one another and made their way to the Russian Embassy.

Although they had an appointment, they were kept waiting in the foyer for about twenty minutes before being called. There they chatted about the possibilities of a successful outcome. Eventually they were ushered into a room by a severe-looking, stony-faced secretary, who introduced them to a senior official. It was too much to expect that they would see the actual ambassador himself, but at least they were here and hadn't been turned away.

"Hello, my name is Ivan Steningrav. Pleased to meet you… Mr. Blake and Mr. Stanhope, I believe?"

"Yes, that's us."

They shook hands, then Mr. Steningrav buzzed through to his secretary. "Please do take a seat; make yourselves comfortable. My secretary will bring some coffee and biscuits for us." They took their seats and looked anxiously at the official. He seemed pleasant enough.

"I've read through your letter again," he said. "I hope that you have more documentation to substantiate this claim."

"Yes, we do," said George. "Please, take a look at these."

George handed him a file containing various documents, which gave all the details of Jack's father and mother: her German Jewish roots, the inheritance, the family names and the address in Berlin, stolen by the Nazis. There was also a written statement from Herr Grüber, together with some photographs provided by him, as well as the name of the Russian officer who had led Aaron away. Furthermore, there were details of the depot he was taken to for questioning, from which he never returned. Additionally, there was a report from John Sullivan, of the British consulate in Berlin, clarifying all of this. George Stanhope said that he felt confident there was nothing to prevent an investigation into the whereabouts of Aaron Goldberg.

The secretary brought coffee and biscuits, which she served while Ivan Steningrav read through the documents. It took quite a while, so they helped themselves to more coffee.

Eventually he closed the file, and his face broadened into a smile.

"Leave all this with me. I will contact you when I have some information. It may take some time, but I feel sure we can locate Aaron Goldberg and, with the evidence you have provided here, we can get him released. He has obviously been done a great disservice. Those were difficult times, you know. Often, the officers just didn't want extra responsibility; they felt they had enough on their hands, supervising the ex-Nazis."

"Yes, indeed. I'm sure there was a lot of confusion," said George, charitably.

"Well, I will get my secretary to make copies of these documents, so you can have the originals back for safekeeping. Be assured that I will do everything I can to help you."

"Thank you very much, Mr. Steningrav."

He buzzed through again and handed the documents to his stony-faced secretary, who went off to make copies. Once she had returned with the originals, they bade farewell and left the embassy, thanking Ivan Steningrav for his time and help.

"Well, that went better than I thought it would," said Jack. "He seems very nice, and extremely helpful."

"Yes, he was. So we now just have to wait. How long that will be, goodness only knows!"

George Stanhope returned to his bank in Manchester and Jack returned to his office at the charity. Once there, he made a few phone calls to Joe and Clare, Andrew and José, giving them an update on everything.

Days turned into weeks, then weeks into months...

José moved in with Andrew, but only for occasional weekends, as he had to take responsibility for the family business in Spain.

Jack scoured the mail every day, looking for a likely letter from Manchester, Berlin, London or even Russia – who knew? The family had just about given up hope of any news from the Russian embassy.

Bzzzzzzz!

"Yes, Josie?"

"Mr. Blake, there's a Mr. George Stanhope on the line for you, from Manchester."

"Put him through, Josie, put him through… Hello, George!"

"Hello, Jack. I've had some news… but it's not good."

Chapter 17

1947

BERLIN

"YOU ARE A spy! A traitor! You are trying to claim a house that is now the property of the Soviet Union!" spat the harsh-looking general – another ghastly customer sat behind a desk – while Aaron stood trembling, flanked by two soldiers.

"No, sir! I used to live in that house. The documents your officer has will prove that: there is a photograph of myself and my family; there is my birth certificate; a letter from my father... I am not lying."

"You will be deported to the Gulag system of labour camps, where you will serve the Soviet Union and make amends for your betrayal."

"No, please! I am not a traitor; I am innocent! I just need to work and make a living."

"Well, where you are going, you will certainly work!"

The other guards laughed at this, and dragged a crying Aaron away. He was thrust into a cell.

He sobbed, not believing how things had turned out.

He was given hard, stale, black Russian bread and ice-cold water, and left alone in a cold, damp prison cell.

The next day, another train arrived...

Oh, God, not another train journey!

At least this was not a cattle truck, and there was some warmth. The carriages were filled with other "prisoners", who spoke among themselves. Some were actually Soviet prisoners of war, released from the Nazi death camps; these Russian soldiers were considered traitors, because they had allowed themselves to be arrested, instead of fighting on the front line. Others were Polish, and were seen as having helped the Nazi machine. One or two, like himself, were German – for them the guards had no sympathy at all.

The journey took days to reach the Gulag system of camps. Upon arrival, they were unloaded, given prison clothing, directed to barracks and given bunk beds.

Still, it was four-star accommodation compared with Auschwitz. But that didn't alter the fact that once again he had lost his freedom – goodness knew what brutality was in store for him.

Yet again, Aaron vowed that he would survive another Hell, and find a way out of this unjust situation. He would not give up.

He quickly made friends with a Polish Jew, about the same age as himself. His name was Benjamin, and he had been given a *Certificate of Freedom* when liberated from Treblinka, but it had been stolen from him by a Nazi guard, who had dressed in prison clothes to avoid execution. With no papers for identification, he had been sent to this labour camp.

The daily work schedule revolved around building a train track. Work started early in the morning and went on until sunset. The food was rather better than Auschwitz, and thick clothing warded off the low temperatures. Rumour had it that there were hundreds of these camps in the Gulag, and no one really knew where in the world they were.

Benjamin introduced Aaron to some other young prisoners, with similar sad stories, and they bonded together well. The guards were not sadistic, but would not tolerate laziness; they were kept working hard all day, with just breaks for drinks, food and toilet needs.

They talked about escape, but not knowing where they were, and with no money, no papers and no food, it seemed impossible.

The railway line they were creating was alongside an already completed track; one day, they were taken by complete surprise when a train passed them. They stopped work for a while and watched as it went by, showering them with snow. It was not long before the guards were shouting at them to get back to work.

Later that night, in the barracks, they discussed the possibility of escape. The train was their chance! If it passed through again, perhaps they could jump onto the last carriage, conceal themselves, and jump off when they approached civilization. It was a glimmer of hope, which kept them all going.

However, the trains were infrequent and passed through too swiftly; it would be virtually impossible to board one. There was also the possibility that the guards would look their way and shoot.

So, the days became weeks, the weeks became months, and the months became years…

Will I ever get out of this hell? thought Aaron.

Chapter 18

1965

LONDON

BZZZZZZ…

"Hi, Josie, what is it?"

"Your wife is on the phone."

Jack groaned. "Okay, Josie, put her through."

Myra didn't wait for him to say anything; "Jack, I need to speak to you, urgently!"

"What is it now, Myra? Man trouble again?"

"Just get here as soon as you can, please!"

Jack put the phone down and wondered what was up with Myra. It couldn't be money. Had she picked up with an undesirable, and got in trouble?

He buzzed Josie and asked if she would deal with any calls, and make appointments for later in the day, or the day after. He promised that he would be back as soon as he could. He then left for Myra's house. He wondered if Andrew would be there.

"What's up, Myra?"

"Jack, I'm not well. I've been to the doctor, he sent me to the hospital and I've had tests. The results came back today: I've got cancer and it's terminal. There's nothing they can do."

Jack was stunned. He looked at her and opened his arms for an embrace. Surprisingly, she fell into his arms and sobbed. He held her tightly.

When she had calmed down, she said: "I know I've been horrible to you, and led a bad life. I'm sorry – really, truly sorry. I wish I'd taken your advice and found counselling, or therapy, whatever… Do you think this is a punishment for my behaviour?"

"It doesn't work like that, Myra. Just remember that I've never stopped loving you, and I will be beside you through this, all the way."

"I don't deserve you. I really don't."

"What about Andrew?"

"I'll tell him when I can find the right time."

"Do you want me to be there, or even to tell him for you?"

"Well, thanks to my venomous tongue, he doesn't want to have anything to do with you, so that might complicate his feelings. No, leave it to me; I'll tell him."

Over the next three months, Myra slowly deteriorated, and eventually went into a nearby hospice for full-time care.

Jack and Joe made a rota of visits, so that Andrew would only be there either on his own, or with his Uncle Joe and Auntie Clare.

Seeing her die like this was devastating, and made them all feel sorry, but their main concern was Andrew. Joe and Clare did everything they could to bolster him and keep him positive. For all her faults she had been a wonderful mother to him, but it was hard to forget how she had behaved, and deprived Andrew of a father figure in his life. The lies, the deceit, the squandering of money on men and the good times all pointed to a mental health condition, but even so it was hard to accept. In spite of all of it, they wanted her to be out of pain and not suffering.

It was alarming how quickly she deteriorated. Before long, Andrew was keeping vigil at her deathbed.

When she was at the point of death, the hospital chaplain came and gave her the last rites. He was kind enough to stay in the corridor outside and, at a nod from the nurse, went back into the ward to comfort Andrew, who was crying like a baby. Andrew gave him Joe and Clare's number, and they made their way to the hospice to put him back together again. Before leaving, they phoned Jack to tell him.

On the day of the funeral, Jack sat at the back of the church and kept his head down, not to draw attention to himself. The close family knew why, of course, and most of Myra's acquaintances didn't know Jack, anyway.

His parish priest from Manchester had always kept in touch, as a family friend, and it was arranged that he would take the service. Jack told him what he was doing, and Father Brian said that he would not draw attention to Jack, but rather concentrate on Andrew. Father Brian gave the eulogy, very cleverly avoiding any mention of Myra's colourful life, while at the same time not canonizing her as a saint.

Joe and Clare sat with Andrew in the front pew. He was very strong throughout the ceremony, but burst into tears as the coffin was taken out of the church, before he, Joe and Clare followed it. Jack looked the other way and held back the tears.

After the interment at the cemetery the reception was held in Myra's house, where Andrew had arranged for caterers to provide an exceptional buffet, with champagne and wine – only the best for his mother. He managed to speak, raising a glass of champagne to a wonderful mother, and his Uncle Joe toasted her as well, with some childhood memories of his sister, before her wayward life caused so much hurt. He told them of Cardiff, in South Wales, where they were born – a place called Splott – and how she had one day found out where their mother kept the sherry. On some evenings she would come into Joe's bedroom with crisps and sherry, and they would get quite tipsy. That was Myra!

Joe tried to persuade Andrew to move back to his mother's house in exclusive Kensington, but he said he liked his apartment and it was near to the boutique, avoiding public transport. He did say, however, that he would not rush into selling her property.

Andrew couldn't help wondering about his father, and how he could have stayed away from the funeral! What sort of a waster was he, womanizing and deserting his son and wife? Joe tried to encourage him to put the past behind him and forget all of that, suggesting that harbouring bitterness would only turn him into a sour person. Fortunately, his boutique business was doing so well in the swinging 'sixties, he was kept busy, and had little time to dwell on things.

Then, one day, about a year later, a letter arrived. It was from his father…

Chapter 19

1966

LONDON

"SO, GEORGE, TELL me, what's not good about the news you have?" said Jack, on the phone to George Stanhope.

"Well, there's a system of labour camps in the Soviet Union called the Gulag – there are hundreds of these camps. The Russian embassy has come back to me confirming that Aaron Goldberg is detained in one of these camps, but are not sure which one."

"They're as bad as the Nazis!" Jack fumed. "A country liberated from the tyranny of the tsars, my foot! They need another revolution. Andrew told me how grim and uninviting the eastern sector of Berlin was. We need an iron curtain to keep them out!"

"Well, we have to keep calm. If we start throwing accusations at them, we may lose their support; the embassy will just shut us out and we won't get anywhere. They're going to contact the Central Bureau of Administration to see if they can locate which camp Aaron Goldberg is detained at but, in the meantime, they've suggested we write to them as well, with copies of all the documentation we have. Ivan Steningrav said that, between the Russian embassy through him, and ourselves, two enquiries about the same man might put a bit of pressure on them. In fact, he said that we should try and get some support from the Home Office. I have to say he was extremely helpful."

"I'll do that," said Jack. "I have contacts there, through the charity. When we have refugees on our hands, we have to go through certain procedures via them. They owe me a few favours."

"Great, let me know how you get on. In the meantime, I'll post copies of these documents to you, so you can put together a portfolio and send it to them. Is that alright?"

"Fine."

Two days later, the documents arrived and Jack put a portfolio together. He telephoned the Home Office and spoke to someone he had dealt with often in the past, explaining the situation and telling the whole story. They wanted to see the portfolio, and asked Jack to drop it off to them.

The following day, he went to the Home Office and handed over the portfolio to the person he had spoken to. He was invited into the office and given coffee and biscuits, as the clerk read through the documents, before deciding to show them to the Home Secretary.

"How long can you wait?"

"I have to be back at the charity for a meeting at four," explained Jack, "so I'm okay for a bit."

"He's in a meeting right now, but it should be coming to an end very soon. Why don't you pop out and get yourself a bite to eat, then come back before one o'clock; he'll be off for lunch then."

"I'll do that."

Jack amused himself by going to one of the new places called Wimpy bars. They had been growing in popularity with the youngsters, and more and more of them were opening in cities and towns. He couldn't believe how quickly the food was produced and he really enjoyed the cheeseburger and chips, washed down with a reasonable paper cup of tea. Soon, it was time to return to the Home Office.

The clerk greeted him in the foyer and said that he'd shown everything to the Home Secretary, who was very helpful: he had written a cover letter on official Home Office headed notepaper, to the effect that he hoped the Soviet officials would cooperate in this scandalous miscarriage of justice, which he had signed.

Jack was elated, and couldn't wait to tell George and the rest of the family.

When he returned to his office, he rang everyone. They all agreed that, if Aaron was located, someone must go to Russia to meet him, and bring him safely over to Britain.

It was a waiting game. Andrew could well imagine the

bureaucracy involved: the number of phone calls, the documents to be read, stamped and signed… He thought back to Berlin.

José declared that it could never be worse than Spain. He told the tale of when he needed medication for his grandmother, Maria, who had been taken ill on holiday in Galicia. Even though it was the same country, she nevertheless had to have the doctor sign and stamp all the prescriptions, and had to be "actualized" as a person living in Murcia Province and not Galicia. After some weeks, she had her money back for the prescriptions, even though she was part of the health system in Spain. *Madre Mia!*

"Gosh, I thought Britain was diabolical," said Andrew.

"Oh, no; it is a great skill with officials in España: stamping documents. I often wonder if they have to have a degree in it!"

They all laughed.

"On a serious note, though, I just hope he's still alive," said Andrew.

"Yes, the thought of a Siberian labour camp doesn't give much hope," said José.

"Well, I've done a bit of research," said Jack: "some of these camps hold political prisoners and serious offenders; they are practically worked to death! However, most are glad to have slave labour to boost the economy of their 'wonderful' communist dream! I can't imagine that Aaron is classed as a political prisoner."

"Well, they did accuse him of being a traitor," said José.

"Yes, but they could never prove that. I believe it was all down to the frustration of a brainless Russian officer, who didn't want the hassle of having to contact the authorities: imagine the paperwork; the German work gang having to be supervised by someone else; the bureaucracy involved, asserting Aaron as the rightful owner of number thirteen… No, it was easier to do away with him."

"Even so," said Andrew, "I'd trust them as much as I would a snowball in the desert! Look at the way that monster Brezhnev behaves, and that idiot Khrushchev before him! We nearly had a nuclear war!"

About two weeks later, Jack received a phone call from the clerk at the Home Office.

"Jack, they have located Aaron Goldberg."

Chapter 20

1943

SPLOTT, CARDIFF

"MAM, I'M OFF to the dance at the church hall. See you later."

"Be careful, love: those G.I.s are all over the place. You know what they're all saying: they're 'over here, overpaid and oversexed'!"

"Oh, Mam, for goodness' sake! This is the church hall I'm going to! I don't think Father Harold is going to allow blatant sex on the dancefloor!"

"Well, just saying take care, that's all!"

"See you later."

So, Myra headed off to St. German's Church Hall. Her mother Blodwen had worshipped there all her life, but Myra had lapsed a little.

On the way to the church hall she called for her friend Anwen, who lived very close by, in Metal Street. Together they made their way to the dance.

"I wonder if there'll be any G.I.s there," said Anwen.

"I hope so! I've seen some of them around; they're absolutely gorgeous! I wouldn't mind being swept off my feet and taken back to America, when this stupid war is over!" said Myra.

"I know. I'm fed up with it: the rationing, the bombs… In these last couple of weeks they've tried to destroy Cardiff Docks! Bloody Germans! Who do they think they are?"

"I saw toilet paper on sale in the market yesterday, with Hitler's face printed on every sheet! I bought some. It's silly, I know, but I feel like: *yes, that's all you deserve, you shitty little bastard!*"

They howled laughing, and reached the doors of the church hall. Inside, they quickly joined some of their friends and sat with them, ogling the G.I.s, who were grouped together on the other side of the hall. Their dream had come true: there was a large gang of them at a table! The boys quickly noticed them. Of course, Myra stood out, with her stunning good looks. The girls giggled, as they saw the boys talking and gesturing amongst themselves.

Eventually, one of the soldiers boldly walked over. He looked like a film star. He made his way directly to Myra and asked for a dance. The very forward young lady didn't normally blush, but on this occasion she went bright red.

"Well, alright, but I'm not very good at dancing."

"You'll be fine; I'll lead you around the dancefloor. Just hold on tight!"

Myra didn't need any more encouragement. Hold on tight? She certainly would do to this Adonis!

The rest of the girls raised their eyebrows, but took it as the norm that, whenever they went out, Myra was always the first to get off with a boy. It didn't put them off, as they made eyes at the remaining group of lads on the other side of the hall. Eventually, they were all partnered off.

The evening passed quickly, and before long the dance was called to a halt. Father Harold went up onto the stage and, using the microphone, bade them all farewell, wishing them a safe journey home.

"Can I walk you home?" offered Hank.

"Yes, but only as far as the corner of the street; if my mother sees you, she'll go wild! We've all been warned about you lot, you know!"

"Oh yes: 'over here, overpaid and oversexed!' I know all about it," said Hank. "The trouble is, we're so far from home and it's nice to have some comfort. I really like you, Myra. Can I see you again?"

"Of course, silly! When?"

"Can I meet you in the café opposite the church hall, at seven tomorrow night?"

"Yes, okay. Where shall we go?"

"The movies?"

"Wow, I haven't been to the pictures in ages!"

Hank laughed; he thought it very funny how the British called them "pictures" and not movies. "Pictures are things you find in a photo album!" he said.

"Well, I guess they're moving pictures – isn't that how they were described when they first came out? What's showing, anyway?"

"*Gone with the Wind*."

Myra couldn't contain herself; "Oh, is that the one with the gorgeous Clark Gable in it?"

"Yeah, but he ain't that special. He's only a regular dude."

"I'll have to lie to my mother and tell her I'm going with Anwen. I'll make sure she supports my alibi."

"Wouldn't it be easier if we came clean, and you introduced me to your mom?"

"Well, perhaps, but not just yet."

So began a relationship between Hank and the gorgeous Myra. It lasted for weeks, until Hank was told by his superiors that they would be posted to the coast.

One day, Myra plucked up the courage to tell her mother that she'd been dancing with a G.I. at the church hall. She said that all the other girls went, and they each had a G.I. "friend".

"I know, Myra. I'm not stupid. Anwen's mother caught sight of her, being dropped off at the corner of the street by one of them. So, she went to the presbytery and enquired when the next dance was; she wanted to confront Anwen and make sure that she kept safe. When the housekeeper told her, she thanked her and added: 'Anwen really enjoyed the dance last night.' To which Mrs. Jones replied: 'There wasn't one last night, love. She must have got her wires crossed.' She got something crossed alright, that was for sure!

"Just be careful, love. I don't want you getting a broken heart – or worse."

Myra eventually brought Hank home and, although she was very nervous, it all went well. Hank was extremely polite and, with his film star looks, Blodwen was really taken with him. In the end, Hank could do no wrong.

"When shall we meet next?" said Hank, at the door.

"Tomorrow. You can come to the house; Mam's off to the Mothers' Union!"

"What's that? It sounds like a vigilante group!"

"Well, it is… kind of; you don't want to mess with them, I can tell you. They'd make a nun feel guilty!"

So, Hank came over, after Blodwen had gone to the Mothers' Union. They couldn't believe their luck, having a comfy sofa, a warm fire and nibbles from the pantry. They kissed and cuddled, and one thing led to another...

Chapter 21

1966

SIBERIA, RUSSIA

"HEY, YOU, JEWBOY, the commandant wants to see you. Now!" shouted one of the guards.

Aaron panicked. What was this all about? He hadn't done anything wrong. He had always worked hard and obeyed orders. He made his way to the commandant's hut. Taking off his cap, he entered gingerly and spoke politely.

"The guard said you wanted to see me, sir."

"Come in and sit down. Don't worry; you haven't done anything wrong. It looks like you have a guardian angel! Some British people have been making enquiries about you for quite some time. It seems that you were arrested falsely and the story you gave in Berlin is true, after all."

Aaron couldn't believe his ears. He wondered if this was a trick. "Are you sure, sir?"

"Yes, I'm sure; my superiors have verified everything. I have here a release permit, valid identification papers and some money for you. A train will pass through here tomorrow and we have ordered it to stop. You will board the train and leave it when you get to Moscow. Here is the address of a hotel in Moscow, where you will meet two British people: father and son Jack and Andrew Blake. They are relatives of yours."

Aaron couldn't speak for a moment. When he did, he explained that he didn't think anyone from his family had survived Auschwitz. He had seen his father brutally beaten to death, and the fate of his mother and Rachel was that of millions of others: gas.

"It's something to do with your grandmother's sister. So, look out for the train tomorrow and come here, so I can explain everything to the conductor."

"Yes, sir. Thank you, sir!"

Aaron walked back to his workmates and explained what had happened. They were astonished, but elated. It gave them hope that someone can actually get released from this hell! He told them he would miss them all, and never forget their friendship. They begged him to make enquiries on their behalf, too, when he was finally free, and he promised that he would. He knew their stories, and the injustices meted out to them – especially Benjamin, with whom he had become very close friends.

He had a sleepless night, and couldn't work things out. Two British people who were relatives? He knew his great-aunt Rebecca had moved to England and married an Englishman, but she had died years ago. When mad Adolf came to power, they didn't hear from them again; Christmas cards stopped coming, which was funny, because they were Jews anyway. His dad Rueben had assumed that it was difficult for mail to get through to Nazi Germany – then, when the war started, it became utterly impossible, of course. Aaron couldn't sleep at all, tossing and turning.

The next day, at noon, a train came to a halt on the completed line, next to where he had been working with his mates. He duly went to the commandant's hut, still wondering if it was all a trick.

The commandant came out and ushered him toward the train's conductor. A conversation ensued and the conductor nodded, shrugged, then looked at Aaron and smiled, offering gestures of reassurance to the commandant. Then, Aaron was put on the train.

The commandant shook his hand and said how sorry he was that such a miscarriage of justice should have occurred. He assured Aaron that the officer responsible for his false arrest would be severely punished when he was found. He simply had to delve into the documentation regarding his false arrest, and it would only be a matter of time before the said officer would be located. He would probably end up taking Aaron's place on the work gang!

The train held very few passengers, but they were all well dressed and appeared quite wealthy. There were husbands with wives, and single men who were obviously businessmen. There were also young people, who looked to be university students.

Aaron was astonished. No wonder the train whizzed through at such alarming speed: they wouldn't want the passengers to see the prisoner work gangs! He wondered what they had thought when it stopped now, and what they considered him to be. He decided to move to a seat farther back, not to look at any of them. Any time he made eye contact, he would look down and keep himself to himself, until they reached Moscow.

The journey seemed endless, and all he could do was contemplate this new situation. Who were these people? Was this a trick, to further ruin his life? He didn't know much about the British, other than that they had formed part of the Allied invasion at the end of the war, and were more tolerable than the Soviets. Did they have concentration camps in Britain, he wondered. How did they know about his great aunt? He pondered… and worried.

He soon fell asleep, to the melodious sound and movement of the train along the tracks.

He awoke with a start at the sound of the train's hooter. The train was slowing down, and was engulfed by the steam from the engine. He looked out of the window: indeed, they had reached Moscow.

He looked at his poor clothing and decided to hold back, so that the other passengers could leave the train first. When the way was clear, he stepped onto the platform. His Russian was not very good – only what he had learnt in the camp – and he didn't want to draw attention to himself by speaking to strangers, so he headed toward the conductor, who knew his situation, and asked for directions to the hotel. The conductor was kind enough to draw a map on the back of an old ticket, complete with street names. The name of the hotel was Hotel National. The conductor told him it had been one of the imperial palaces before the revolution.

Aaron thanked him and made his way there, following the map and trying to look for the street names. He made a few wrong turns and had to ask once or twice, showing the name of the street on his little map.

Eventually he sighted the hotel. It was enormous and very grand! He could quite clearly see that it had indeed once been a palace.

He was extremely nervous about entering in his shabby clothes, and walked up and down the street several times, before plucking up the courage to approach it. People stared at him, thinking that he was a beggar, and he realized that he could easily be picked up by the police if he hung around any longer – then he would be back at square one. Eventually, he plucked up the courage and entered the hotel.

He went to the reception desk and asked if there were two British gentlemen by the name of Blake staying at the hotel. The clerk looked at him with great suspicion, noting immediately his shabby clothes. He went off and spoke to the manager.

Oh dear, this isn't going to work out, Aaron thought. *They are probably about to throw me out.*

Fortunately, the manager had been informed by Jack and Andrew of Aaron's situation. He came over and shook the German's hand, to the astonishment of the clerk. He told Aaron to take a seat in the foyer, while he rang through to the rooms the Blakes were staying in. In the meantime, he instructed a waiter to bring some hot, black Russian tea, which was served on a silver platter with biscuits.

Aaron couldn't take it all in. The last time he had eaten a biscuit was when his mother had made them as a treat for Passover. That was an age ago!

The manager returned and said that Mr. Blake and his son Andrew were making their way down to the foyer, and would not be long. It seemed like ages, no doubt because of the size of the place. Eventually, two men who looked to be evidently father and son came down the palatial staircase, and made their way toward him.

He stood up, and thanked the god he had lost faith in that he had learnt some English at school in Berlin, before the Nazis came to power. Although he had forgotten a lot of it, he felt sure that he could make himself understood.

"Hello, Aaron. I'm Jack and this is my son, Andrew. We've been searching for you for a long time. We are so glad to meet you."

Aaron croaked: "I'm sorry that I am so confused by your visit, and at my release from the Gulag; I have worried that it is all a mistake! I'm also sorry for my shabby clothes and dishevelled appearance."

"Don't worry about any of that," said Andrew. "We'll sort you out in no time at all. What's much more important is that we explain how all of this has come about. There's no need to worry about anything; you are a free man, at last! Everything is fine."

Aaron started to cry.

Andrew took hold of him and hugged him, like a brother.

"We're related, you know, so you are with family!" he smiled. "Your grandmother and mine were sisters. Now, let's settle ourselves somewhere, and we'll explain everything to you."

"I'm so confused," said Aaron.

"Don't worry, Aaron; all will be revealed," said Jack.

Jack spoke to the manager, and they were taken to a private lounge on the next floor. Jack ordered some refreshments and they settled down on plush sofas. Aaron felt so out of place, in his shabby clothes with the well-dressed Blakes, in such plush surroundings.

Jack and Andrew explained everything to the stunned man. They told him all about Jack's father and his wife Rebecca, who was Aaron's great aunt. They told him about the bank's instructions. They explained that Andrew had been to Berlin to look for him, and had met Herr Grüber. They also said they had managed to get a visa for him to return to Britain with them, and that they hoped he would. Aaron said he would be happy to; he had nowhere else to go! When it had sunk in about the family fortune, and that Jack's solicitors would arrange for him to be reimbursed, he felt as if it was all a dream.

They talked for ages about Auschwitz, and the horrors he had witnessed there. Then, he went into detail about the interrogation in Berlin, and how distraught he had been that he was going straight into captivity, yet again. He told them about the Gulag system, and how it could be almost impossible to find anyone there; most would die in captivity as enforced workers: slaves! The loss of his loved ones and his home was the only thing which had kept him going; he wanted to bring justice to this nightmare.

"Well, Aaron, you will certainly have the opportunity to do that now. You are a very rich man… and free at last!"

Andrew said that he would take Aaron shopping, to kit him out in some new clothes. They wouldn't be as trendy as his stylish Carnaby Street garb, but at least they would be new and clean. Jack went off to make sure that the room they had booked for him was still available, and booked a table in the restaurant for an evening meal.

*

When Aaron and Andrew returned later with some new clothes, he was shown to his room. It was amazing; it had its own bathroom, a double bed and a fantastic view over the city. He fell on the bed and spread himself out. He laughed. Then he cried.

"Oh, Papa, Mama and Rachel! I hope you are looking down and can see what's happening!" he cried.

Andrew came over, took hold of him and hugged him as he sobbed. "Don't worry, Aaron, everything is going to be fine. We're cousins, you know; we're family. I know this is so much for you to handle, but take your time. My room is next door and my dad's is across the corridor; if you're worried about anything just give us a shout.

"Now, have a shower, shave and put your new clothes on; dinner is at seven p.m. When you are ready, knock on my door, we'll call for Dad and we'll all go down to the restaurant together."

Aaron wiped his eyes. "Thank you so much!"

Aaron decided to have a bath rather than a shower: showers were reminiscent of Auschwitz! When they were herded into communal shower rooms, and told they were going to be deloused, they were never sure if water or gas was going to come out. Besides, he could wallow in a warm bath and soak away the pains and sorrows, the memories and the fears. It was luxurious! Piping hot water! Such a change from the cold water in a trough at the camp. There were soap, shaving tools and an abundance of towels and mirrors.

After a long soak, he looked at the watch Aaron had bought him and realized that he needed to get dressed. Although Andrew had teased him that he looked very 1950s, alongside his own modern 'sixties clothing, he rather liked what he saw.

As he looked in the full-length mirror, he could see his father looking back. He suddenly felt pained and wanted to cry again. How delighted his father would be, that his ploy had worked: putting evidence behind the dresser in the kitchen, at their home in Berlin. If Rueben could see him now, he would be so appeased.

He pulled himself together, finished dressing and left the room, to knock on Andrew's door.

"Wow, you look very smart, Aaron. You're going to catch the eye of many a young lady!"

Together they knocked on Jack's door, and the three of them made their way down to the restaurant.

The restaurant looked like a ballroom, and Jack said that it probably had been, when it was a palace. The décor, the chandeliers, the carpets… everything spoke of grandeur and elegance – so out of context with Communist Russia!

"This grandeur doesn't seem to fit in with the revolution, and the communist ideal of all having everything in common," said Andrew.

"Well, it's probably just for the tourists' benefit, to make it look as if Russia is prospering," said Jack.

"Careful, Dad! Keep your voice down or *we* might end up in the Gulag system!"

Aaron was stunned, and shook his head in disbelief, as Jack and Andrew just grinned at each other.

They were shown to a table and given menus. Jack chose a very expensive red wine, while Andrew struggled with his Russian phrasebook, to try and decipher the available options on the extensive menu. In the end, they chose soup, steaks and trifle – or so they hoped! In fact, the food was delicious. It was a Russian recipe, and wasn't anything like that of standard British fare, but stunning, nevertheless. Aaron enjoyed every mouthful.

"I haven't eaten like this since I was twelve!" he said. "Once the Nazis started to deprive us of our rights and citizenship, food became a scarcity. After we were hauled out of our home and beaten with rods by those thugs, we never saw a proper meal again."

"Well, there's plenty more opportunities for fine wining and dining now," said Jack. "You deserve it!"

"Tomorrow we travel to London," said Andrew.

"Oh, I always wanted to go to London as a boy. My dad Rueben always promised us that he'd take us there one day – before that murderer became chancellor of Germany."

"Yes, it's frightening how politics can work out sometimes. Just look at Spain: another murderer called Franco."

"I don't know much about that," said Aaron; "I've been hidden away in camps since I was fourteen."

"You'll learn," said Jack. "He was another dictator – best friend of that dickhead Adolf!"

Chapter 22

1943

SPLOTT, CARDIFF

AN AIR RAID siren was going off.

"Oh, those bloody Germans!" said Myra. "I wish I could fly a 'plane and flatten Berlin! Bastards!"

"Come on, love; to the shelter, as quick as we can," said Blodwen. "Oh, I just need to get my book. Goodness knows how long we'll be in there for this time!"

"Hurry up, Mam. How you can read with all that going on beats me, anyway!"

Blodwen hurried upstairs for her book and handbag, while Myra waited by the front door, ready to make a dash for it with her mother, to the church grounds, where there was a communal shelter.

Too late! The house was hit!

Myra ran out onto the street, screaming.

Others, who had been a little slow leaving their homes, also came out screaming. The middle four houses of the street's terraced row had been hit. In no time at all, fire engines could be heard approaching. Myra tried to go back in for her mother, but one of the neighbours pulled her back.

"It's not possible, my love; the whole of the upstairs is blazing. She's not going to make it, I'm afraid. And if you go in there you'll be lost, as well!"

"Oh, Mam, why did you have to go back for that wretched book?!" Myra sobbed uncontrollably, in the arms of her neighbour.

The fire engines arrived, along with an ambulance, and they got to work immediately. The bombers had by now gone. They were just passing over on their way to the docks, and had dropped a few along the way.

Then, for one moment, Myra forgot her tears, as the most handsome man stepped out of the ambulance. She couldn't take her eyes off of him, but quickly came to her senses when she realized that he was talking to her, asking her if there was anyone in the house.

"Yes, my mother. She went back in for a book."

"Well, the firemen have gone in now; they'll bring her out. Hopefully we can save her. My name is Jack, by the way."

"Oh, please, God, please let her be alright."

Once they had quelled the fire, they searched the house. One of the firemen came out, cradling Blodwen in his arms. Myra dashed forward, but Jack held her back, saying that he would look at her first.

"Too late I think, Jack," said the fireman. "I'll lay her in the ambulance and you can check her over."

It took no time at all for Jack to certify that she was dead. He turned to Myra and said: "I'm sorry, love. She hasn't made it."

Myra fell into his arms and cried bitterly. Jack comforted her, telling her that her mother would have died of the fumes, and not felt any pain from the burns.

When she had stopped crying, Jack explained that she would have to go to the church hall, as a help centre had been set up there, for those affected by the bombing. There would be others there who had been made homeless; arrangements were being made for them to be rehoused elsewhere. He offered to take her there, before taking Blodwen's body to the hospital, for the doctor to sign a death certificate.

As she was treated in the ambulance, Myra spoke quietly: "You're English, aren't you, Jack? That's not a Welsh accent."

"Yes, I'm from Manchester, but I was posted to Cardiff, to help with the war effort here. It's pretty hectic – and dangerous, too – but if a life can be saved it's all worth it. I'm so sorry we couldn't save your mother."

"Oh, if only she hadn't gone back upstairs, to get a book to read in the air-raid shelter, she would still be here! I don't know what's going to happen now, I really don't. It'll take ages for the house to be sorted. All our belongings are destroyed!"

"Don't worry, you're not the only one in this plight. The authorities are doing their very best to get people rehoused and back to some sort of normality."

When they reached the church hall, Jack said: "If you want to meet up sometime, I'd like that. If there's anything I can do, to help things along, it might make things easier for you."

"Oh yes, please, that would be very kind of you! I'm all of a dither, and there's so much to think about: a funeral, house insurance..."

"Well, here's the number of the ambulance station where I'm billeted. Once the authorities have accommodated you, give me a ring and we'll arrange to meet up. Tomorrow I have a day off, so I can help you with a few things, if you'd like."

"Oh, thank you so much, Jack! You're an angel."

"Try not to worry now."

What a gorgeous girl, Jack thought to himself; *she's stunning!*

Myra stepped out of the ambulance and walked to the church hall. There she saw people she knew, from the other bombed houses, who were in the same plight as herself.

Near the door was a desk with some officials from the War Damage Commission behind it, and she was told to register with them. After giving all the necessary information – name, age, address, mother's name, insurance company, job, etc. – Myra was sent to another desk where, after filling in more details, she was given the address of an area on the other side of Cardiff, where they were erecting "prefabs", under the Temporary Housing Programme for bomb victims. The address was Llandinam Crescent, Gabalfa. She was told that, once the repair work was done on the house, she would be able to return. Apparently the damage was minimal, unlike some areas, where whole streets had been flattened. It often happened that the bombers on their way to Cardiff Docks would drop the odd bomb, just for the hell of it.

Eventually, Myra was then led to the church hall stage. Behind the curtains she found camp beds, where she was told to sleep for the night, before making her way to Gabalfa the next morning. Hopefully there wouldn't be another air raid.

The other people on the stage were her neighbours, from the other six houses bombed in the street – that was a help. They were all very sorry to hear about Blodwen.

It was a sleepless night, interspersed with tears. In the end, with no one able to settle down, they made tea for themselves and talked about the future. All wondered what on Earth a prefab looked like.

"Are they tents, or what?" said one woman.

The next morning, she went back to the house, to see what she could salvage. But the police were on guard, and explained that it was unsafe to enter. Most of the clothing and belongings had been destroyed, anyway. She thought of all her lovely dresses and precious things, but quickly realized that they were nothing at all, compared to the loss of her beloved mother. More tears followed.

She had to use the vouchers she had been given to purchase a few changes of clothes, toiletries and other essentials. Then, she caught a bus to Gabalfa.

On the way to Llandinam Crescent, she could see people going about their everyday business, as if nothing had happened. However, she did notice other streets destroyed by bombs, and wondered how they were coping, and if they had lost loved ones, like her.

When she arrived and got off the bus, she could see lots of small bungalows. She couldn't quite believe it; they looked delightful!

She went to the one which acted as an office and there she handed over her papers. The warden smiled and gave her the key to her prefab. Walking with her, the warden explained that "prefab" was an abbreviation of the word "prefabricated"; the bungalow was not made of traditional building materials, but parts constructed elsewhere, and that allowed them to be erected very quickly. However, they were safe and sound, she promised. Inside, she showed Myra the lounge-cum-dining area, together with the bedroom, small kitchen and bathroom. It was furnished with unmatching items, but looked very cosy.

She thanked the warden, then asked if there was a telephone box nearby.

"Yes, there's one at the end of the street, my dear. I hope you settle in and try to put the trauma you've been through somewhere at the back of your mind. Life has to go on."

The warden then wished her well, and left her to unpack the items she had bought with the vouchers.

'Somewhere at the back of my mind'?! Myra thought, cynically. *How can I put my mother at the back of my mind?*

After unpacking, she made her way to the telephone box and rang the number Jack had given her. When the phone was answered, she asked to speak to him.

"Who shall I say is calling?"

"My name is Myra."

She could hear the person calling for Jack; "There's a Myra on the phone for you."

In no time at all, Jack was speaking to her.

"How are you doing, Myra? I've been thinking about you all night."

"I'm alright, really. I don't care about the house or my belongings; it's my dear mother I miss. What a terrible end for a dear soul."

"I know. Where have they put you?"

"Llandinam Crescent, in a prefab. I've just moved in."

"Okay. I'm not sure where that is, but if you give me a landmark I'll try and find you."

"Well, you need to get the bus to Gabalfa. When I got off I noticed a pub, which I had to walk past to get here. I could meet you there later."

"Good idea; let's say in an hour's time? Don't go in the pub alone, though – you know what people are like about ladies drinking on their own!"

"Ha ha, I know! It's ten-thirty now; I'll come by the pub at eleven-thirty and you can meet me outside."

"What's the name of the pub?"

"The Master Gunner. Sick, really, considering what's happened. So, catch a bus to Gabalfa; you'll pass the pub and can get off the at the next stop."

"Great. See you later."

Chapter 23

1966

SAN JAVIER, SPAIN

"HOLA, PAPÁ, I'M back."

"Hope you had a good flight, son," said Antonio.

"Yes, no problems. The worst part is always the journey from Alicante, on that rickety old bus! I wish there was an airport near here."

"Yes, I know. They are talking about it, with the increase of tourism since Franco has agreed to lift the bikini ban, and hordes want to come here for the sun."

"Well, I'll believe it when I see it."

After they hugged, José said: "I'm going out with some friends tonight, if that's alright, Papá? I know I've only just arrived home, but it was arranged long before I went to London. It's not until later, though, so we can have a good catch up on all that's been happening, before I go."

"That's okay, son; you're not a teenager anymore. Are you going to a dance?"

"Yes, it's in Los Alcázares and it's organized by the church, so it won't go on all night." They both laughed.

José made some coffee, then sat down with his dad and gave him an update on all that had been happening. First was Myra's funeral.

Antonio knew of her death, of course, but didn't feel that he wanted to travel to London for the funeral. He had never quite come to terms with her ideas of abortion, and her sense of relief at the news of José's apparent death. If she'd had her way then a wonderful, handsome, intelligent, caring young man would never have existed! Antonio felt so lucky to have found him, and he knew that José appreciated the years he had spent trying.

José told him that Father Brian had done a great job giving the eulogy – not dwelling on her past, for Andrew's sake, but focusing on her bravery during her illness. Although José knew what his mother had done, he couldn't help feeling sorry for her, and even more so for Andrew, of whom he had become quite fond as a half-brother.

"She had mental health problems, Papá."

"Yes, I know, son. But if your grandmother were alive now, she would tell you how aghast we were at her appalling attitude."

"I know. It gives me the creeps when I think about it."

More intriguing for Antonio was the news of Aaron Goldberg. José filled him in on the heartbreaking story of the young man's further captivity, and all the years of his life wasted. He explained that Jack and Andrew had travelled to Moscow, to bring him back to London. It had been a tricky endeavour, involving the Russian embassy and the British Home Office but, eventually, despite the Cold War, visas had been granted. As Aaron was a citizen of Germany and not the U.S.S.R., it made things a little easier, because he was a resident of Berlin, before it was carved up by the Allies, after the war. This was apparently going to make all the difference, even though his address was now in the Russian sector.

He told Antonio that they had all discussed the fact that the charity would have to be reorganized, because the Blake fortune needed to be in the hands of its rightful heir, Aaron Goldberg. He explained that it was all in the hands of the family solicitor, who was quite confident that an agreeable solution could be found.

"I will return next weekend. Hopefully they will have brought him back by then, so I can meet him and join in the discussion with the solicitor."

"I hope that goes well, son."

José made some seafood paella for lunch, and they relaxed on the terrace with wine.

They discussed how the business was doing so well, and that Julio had proved to be a trustworthy employee, managing things very well, indeed.

Soon, it was time for José to leave and meet his friends.

"There's some tapas in the fridge, Papá. I won't be late. Diego is picking me up in his new car – I think he wants to show it off!"

"What about food for yourself?"

"There's some tapas being served there, so I'll be fine. I ate something on the plane this morning, as well as the paella with you, so I'm okay."

José went to take a shower and put on fresh clothes, which he had got in London – very stylish. Andrew had given them to him, from his boutique. Diego had told him about a girl who would be at the dance with her sister.

Diego and José had made friends when he came to live with his father. Diego's father already worked for the family business and, when he heard José's story, he quickly got his son to befriend the young man. They hit it off, being the same age with similar interests.

You never know, this might be my lucky night, José thought to himself.

A toot on a car horn outside let him know when Diego had arrived.

"Adios, Papá."

"Salud!"

Outside, Diego was sitting in his new sports-car, grinning.

"Wow! Did you rob a bank to buy this?" José gushed.

"It's quite old, actually, and was going for a good price at the garage. So, I saved and saved, and here it is."

In the car, on the way to Los Alcázares, Diego explained that the girls they were meeting were from the nearby village of San Cayetano. José had never been there, so he couldn't pass comment, but understood from Diego that they were a good family, who owned a lot of farmland. In fact, Diego said that quite a lot of vegetables came from there to Antonio's distribution centre, for delivery.

They arrived at the civic centre in Los Alcázares, and were greeted by the priest. Diego introduced José to Father Sebastián.

"Nice to meet you. I expect you attend the church at San Javier."

"Uh... yes," lied José. Well, it wasn't quite a full-bodied lie; they had attended for funerals, weddings and baptisms! Antonio and José had lost touch with the Church, because of José's circumstances and after all that had happened – all thanks to the Church!

"Enjoy yourselves."

"Gracias, Padre."

Then, Diego nearly dragged José into the centre, when he caught sight of the girls.

"Hola, chicas! This is my friend, José. His father buys vegetables from your father's finca."

"Hola," they both said, eyeing up the Adonis that was José.

"This is Isabella and this is Alma."

"Pleased to meet you," said José. He in turn was eyeing up the girls, who could have been Hollywood celebrities. Their sweet faces, perfectly styled hair, chic dresses, stunning high-heeled shoes and slim figures all met with José's approval. *Which one?* It didn't matter; they were both gorgeous. And, they had great personalities, which he would find out as the evening progressed.

The gods decided who was to pair with whom; it transpired that Isabella seemed drawn to Diego, leaving Alma to concentrate on José.

It was a match well made, and they danced the night away, enjoying drinks and tapas. On the stage, a band was playing modern music from Britain. It was very popular; songs of The Beatles, The Rolling Stones and The Kinks were all rendered very well, throughout the evening.

While they were dancing, José said: "I hope we can meet up again."

"Oh, yes, definitely. Why don't you and Diego come to the villa, in San Cayetano. We have a big family get-together every Sunday, and you'll be most welcome. Isabella has already asked Diego. He's willing if you are."

"That sounds great, but shouldn't you ask your parents first?"

"They won't mind. The more the merrier!"

"Okay, if you're sure."

All too soon, Father Sebastián was up on the stage, taking the microphone from the singer. He thanked the band and hoped everyone had enjoyed themselves. He said he looked forward to the next occasion, and told everyone to make sure they bought tickets as the civico could only hold so many people. Nothing was ever advertised properly in Spain, so all would be by word of mouth. "Keep your ears open!" He then wished them all a safe journey home.

As they left the civic centre, Isabella and Alma could see that their father Mateo was waiting in the car. He got out and Diego introduced José, explaining that his father Antonio did business with him.

"Ah, yes, I know Antonio. A fine man." This seemed to please Mateo, who had been scrutinizing José. Still, though, his tanned, wrinkled face showed no emotion, as he embraced José in the traditional way and wished him goodnight.

"I've invited them for lunch on Sunday, Papá. Is that alright?" said Alma.

"Yes, that will be great; your Mama loves cooking," said Mateo. "The more the merrier!" He suddenly looked pleased, perhaps thinking that he would get both girls married off soon!

"Adios, everyone!" he said.

"Salud!" they all replied.

Diego and José got into his sports-car and drove back to San Javier.

"Well, what do you think?" said Diego.

"I'm hooked! Alma is delightful."

"Well, when you went to the toilets, she told her sister that she really liked you and couldn't wait to meet up with you again."

"Well, it's going to be Sunday, so I understand. I'm a bit nervous, meeting her family so soon."

"Don't be: they're great people! Old Mateo is a bit patriarchal, but the rest of the family are really laid back, and they'll adore you. I'll pick you up at one-forty-five; lunch is at two o'clock, but I warn you, it will go on until about five p.m. or later."

"Sounds typically Spanish! I've missed that, spending so much time in Britain. Things are so different there: the weather, the pace of life… And everything is so expensive! They'd charge you for breathing the air in Britain, if they could!" They both laughed.

Diego dropped José off, reminding him that he would be back at quarter-to-two on Sunday.

"Adios, mi amigo."

"Salud!"

Chapter 24

1966

LONDON

JACK, ANDREW AND Aaron landed safely at Heathrow, and went straight to Jack's home. The housekeeper had prepared the guest wing, which included a bedroom, bathroom and sitting room. This would afford Aaron some privacy until available money would allow him to buy his own property.

"My goodness, this is a palace!"

"Well, make yourself at home until we get you sorted. We have an appointment with the solicitor in the morning. Dinner is at seven p.m.; I think Madge, my housekeeper, has rustled up something exciting for you, Aaron – I hope you like it. She delights in catering, and the challenge of German food has given her something to think about."

"You are all so kind. I can't begin to think how I can thank you."

"Nonsense! You have a lot of catching up to do: years of living a normal life, stolen by the Nazis and Soviets."

"Well, it's going to take some getting used to. I was thinking to myself, on the plane coming over, that I have been in captivity as a slave for twenty-three years; I'm now thirty-six!"

"Well, Aaron, we have a saying here in this country, that 'life begins at forty', and you're a little way from that yet. You are family now, and as a family we will do everything possible to help you adjust and get used to life here."

"Thank you so much, Jack."

"Before dinner I want you to meet José, who is Andrew's half-brother, and my late wife's brother Joe, and his wife Clare. I don't want you to meet them tomorrow at the solicitor's; there'll be enough to take in then, without meeting new faces. Is that alright?"

"Okay, that's fine."

"So, as soon as you've unpacked and freshened up, we'll go. It's not far away. I've asked José to be there, so you can meet the three of them at the same time."

When Aaron was ready, they set off in Jack's car to Maida Vale.

Driving through London was quite an experience. He could barely remember driving with his father through Berlin, before the Nazis prevented all Jews from driving and stole their cars.

When they arrived at Joe and Clare's house, Aaron gasped: another palatial property which took his breath away; he felt once again that he was dreaming. It made him think of his comrades in Siberia, and reminded himself of his promise to make investigations on their behalf. This he would certainly do when things were sorted.

The afternoon went well, and Aaron learnt more fully about the family he was now part of. Jack and Andrew had given him a brief outline in Moscow, but now he knew the full story. He heard José's heartbreaking story and learned all about Myra. He couldn't help joking that Myra was like a saint, beside some of the Nazi women he had encountered in the camp. They were hard, heartless creatures; it was difficult to call them females… difficult to call them human, in fact! Apart from the image of his father being beaten to death by a guard, another image he could never get out of his mind was when a Nazi woman had shot a pregnant girl in the stomach, declaring: "Two for the price of one, saving bullets for the Reich!" Her fellow guards had laughed and laughed.

Soon, it was time to return to Jack's house for dinner. Andrew was there.

Madge had prepared a traditional German meal, especially for Aaron, very mindful to avoid pork. There was sauerbraten – a pickled roast beef – together with kartoffelpuffer: shallow pan-fried pancakes, made from grated potatoes, flour, egg and onion. There were also plenty of fresh vegetables. This was followed by Schwarzwälder kirschtorte, a Black Forest gateau, and all washed down with a very expensive Mosel Riesling. Aaron couldn't believe his eyes.

"I haven't eaten food like this since before the Nazis came to power and started restricting our movements, depriving us of our livelihoods and starving us. The days long before we were herded and beaten into lorries and cattle trucks, to end up in Auschwitz."

"Well, I told you Madge had rustled up something special to make you feel at home and welcome," said Jack.

"We're family now, Aaron," said Andrew; "because of your great aunt Rebecca, we have Jewish blood in us, so we are kin – but please don't ask me to give up bacon, and I'm certainly not going to be circumcised!" They all laughed.

"I'm afraid my religious feelings died in that Hell on Earth. We all felt that Yahweh had abandoned us, and I cannot bring myself to even think of keeping the Sabbath or Passover, or anything like that."

"Maybe in time, Aaron," said Jack, "maybe in time."

They enjoyed the evening, with Madge's sumptuous food and plenty of wine. They chatted for ages about life in Berlin, before and after the Nazis. Aaron told them about his comrades in Siberia, and how he had promised to investigate their cases. Jack assured him that, once Aaron was rehabilitated, they would help him in this quest.

The next morning, they headed for the solicitor's office, where a meeting had been arranged with Joe, Clare, José, Jack and Andrew, together with the Charities Commission, as well as George Stanhope from Manchester's National Westminster Bank and, of course, Aaron. After introductions were made, the commissioner spoke first.

"I have spoken with the Charities Board of Governors, and we have come to an agreement regarding this extraordinary turn of events. There is absolutely no doubt in our minds that the inheritance belongs to Herr Goldberg."

"Please, call me Aaron."

"Yes, you are the rightful heir, Aaron, and our lawyers have declared that if you wish to retrieve what belongs to you, then the Blake Charity Foundation will need to be disbanded, and a calculation made of what you would have received, had your parents died of natural causes and Germany not fallen to the Nazis. This will be complicated, but our lawyers insist that it can be done."

Silence…

"No, please! I have been without money, belongings and property for more than twenty-three years; even as a child I only knew hardship, persecution, insults and the struggle for survival. My father would be thrilled to know that the money had been put to such good use, helping the unfortunate."

"Well, perhaps you need to discuss all of this with your newfound family. As far as we are concerned, the ball is in your court."

"Can I ask how much Jack's father inherited?"

"It was a staggering figure: five million pounds," said George.

"Where did it come from?"

"The Credit Suisse Bank."

Aaron thought hard for a moment, then he spoke.

"Yes, the fortune goes way back to my grandfather and his forefathers. There's a lot of money in jewellery. My father managed to whisper to me in the camp one day, when a guard was nowhere near, that if ever I was lucky enough to survive, there was money in two banks: one was the Credit Suisse Bank Group and the other was Bank Lombard Odier. All I would have to do is prove who I was."

The silence ensued…

"Then that means there's another fortune somewhere in Switzerland!" said George.

They all gasped.

"Gosh!" said Andrew.

"Can we have another meeting when I've investigated this, and we'll decide the way forward?" asked George.

They all agreed.

The commissioner said that his work was done; there was no need for him to come again. He had outlined the Charities Commission's legal stance on it all; it was now down to the family and their solicitor how to proceed. He shook hands with everyone and wished Aaron well.

"If the other bank still has the money my father invested, it will be more than enough for me, and your charity can remain as it is," said Aaron. "I have some ideas for a charity of my own."

"Well, don't make any hasty decisions. Let's see what George comes up with."

Chapter 25

1944

SPLOTT, CARDIFF

JACK PROVED TO be a real gem, helping Myra with the funeral, and all the legal things which needed sorting out regarding her mother's will, including endless visits to inspect the restoration of the house. She admitted that she couldn't have done any of it without his help. She was growing very fond of Jack Blake!

The funeral was held at St. German's, and all the neighbours were in attendance. Father Harold conducted the service with great dignity, and Anwen's father gave the eulogy, which Myra had helped to compose. After the service, they all went to the local pub for drinks and sandwiches.

Myra wasted no time in seducing Jack. They made love frequently in her prefab. She really felt that he was the one for her. *If only Mam were alive to meet him, I'm sure she would be thrilled,* she thought to herself.

She and her friends met up regularly and Jack got on well with them all, and their respective boyfriends. Although in the middle of a war, there were good times in between air raids, rationing and Jack's stressful work with the ambulances.

"Will you marry me, Myra?"

"Oh, my gosh! Yes, Jack, I will! When?"

"Well, as soon as I can get some time off and arrange everything."

"Can we live here together?"

"Well, we practically are already! It will be better than the barracks where they've stationed me; it's like a prison there."

"Oh, I'm so excited, Jack. And, when my mother's house is restored, we can move in there."

"There's a bit of bad news there, Myra, I'm afraid: she didn't own the house; it was rented."

"Oh, no! She never said; I always assumed it was ours. Oh, God, Jack, that means I'm homeless!"

"Not exactly, Myra: you have this prefab, and I dare say the council will let you move back in once the house is restored – you'll just have to pay rent, that's all. Things will work out when this wretched war is over, I'm sure."

The wedding took place in St. German's Church, with their friends as witnesses. Being wartime, it was a modest affair. Myra's brother Joe and his wife Clare came – they lived in London, and had always kept in touch with Myra. Unfortunately, Jack's father Harry couldn't come; he suffered from Parkinson's disease and lived in a nursing home in Manchester, where Jack was from. Anwen's boyfriend was the best man and Anwen's father gave Myra away. Anwen was the bridesmaid.

Myra looked stunning in a two-piece suit: typical wartime garb for a bride. The ceremony was simple but very dignified; bride and groom were so happy. Everyone met in a nearby pub afterward, for drinks and sandwiches – a typical wartime reception.

"I want to take you to meet my dad," Jack said, when they were alone. "He's in a nursing home in Manchester, suffering from Parkinson's disease."

"Oh, poor man! Yes, when do you want to go?"

"How about this weekend?"

"Great. Where will we stay?"

"I know a guest house close to the nursing home; it's very comfortable and quite cheap."

"Sounds great, Jack. Can't wait."

They settled into the guest house, ordered some food and decided to go for a walk, just in case the sirens went off. They managed a long walk, during which Jack was able to point out various landmarks to Myra: places of interest to him as a boy growing up. Luckily, there were no German bombers, and they returned to the guest house safely.

After they ordered some drinks at the bar, Myra said: "I've got some news for you, Jack."

"Oh, yes? What's that, love?"

"I'm pregnant."

"My darling, that's wonderful!" He swept her up in his arms. They embraced and kissed passionately. "When is it due?"

"Well, should be about August, I think."

"Let's get a bottle of wine. I'm sure the landlady will let us drink up in our room, when she knows what we're celebrating."

"Yes, let's do that."

In fact, the landlady was delighted, and happily gifted the wine.

The next day they went to the nursing home, and Jack introduced Myra to his father. They seemed to hit it off.

Harry said: "She's a looker, Jack! You know how to pick 'em!"

"He's quite a looker himself," said Myra. "In fact, I can see now where he gets his good looks from!"

"Flattery will get you nowhere, my dear!"

They all laughed.

"Well, Dad, we've got some good news for you: Myra's pregnant. The baby is due in August."

"Oh, that's wonderful news! I'm so pleased for you both. I'll be a grandad, at last! Your gran, my darling Rebecca, would be so proud."

"I know, Dad. She's looking over us, don't you worry!"

Matron came in with tea and cakes, and they enjoyed an afternoon together. When it was time to leave, they made their farewells.

Jack and Myra slipped into Matron's office to ask how his health was. She explained that he was slowly deteriorating.

Andrew was born in 1945 – a bonnie baby; Jack was besotted.

It was a struggle for the three of them, in the small prefab, but they managed. However, Jack couldn't help but notice a change in Myra; she was not the same bubbly, fun-loving character he had fallen in love with. There was something altogether different, and he couldn't put his finger on it. Was this something to be expected after giving birth, he wondered.

"Oh, sweetie, that was the most wonderful sex! You are gorgeous! Where are you from again?"

"Mississippi!"

"I knew one of you lot from Kansas; his name was Hank. He was gorgeous, too."

Chuck looked at Myra's beautiful body and started to become aroused again.

That was when he heard a baby cry.

"What's that?"

"Oh, nothing; it's just my boy. He probably needs feeding."

"You mean you have a baby? You're married?"

"Well, yes. Does that matter?"

"Of course it matters! What do you think you're doing?"

"Oh, I'm just bored with everything, sweetie."

"You've used me! How could you? I thought we were becoming a couple. I need to leave, right now!"

"Suit yourself, sweetie."

Chuck dressed as quickly as he could and fled, slamming the door behind him.

Myra finally got out of bed to feed Andrew, and slipped back into the role of a mother again.

This went on for quite some time, with Jack unaware. Myra brought more and more young men back to the prefab; she just didn't seem to care!

But, as Andrew grew, she knew she would have to be more careful. She had made good friends with the neighbours, and she would often leave the child with them while she met up with different men. All of this happened while Jack was on duty with the Ambulance Service.

It was in December 1946 that he came home early from the ambulance station, as the chief wanted to instruct a new recruit, so it was easier to let Jack have a few hours off. When he entered the prefab, he could hear moans and groans coming from the bedroom.

He thought something was wrong with either Myra or Andrew. Opening the bedroom door, he saw Myra and a young man making love together. He froze.

They hadn't noticed him, and he stared for a moment. Then, trying to regain his composure, he just said: "Enjoying yourselves, are you?"

Myra screamed. The boy jumped out of bed quickly, stumbling as he fumbled to put his clothes on. He was a lot younger than Myra. When he was dressed, he darted past Jack and made his way to the door.

"Shut the door on the way out," said Jack, "and don't come back!"

Myra had gathered the bedclothes around her. She looked shocked.

"Where's the baby?" he demanded.

"He's next door!"

Jack looked at her in disgust. "How long has this been going on? Answer me!"

"This one? Only today."

"You mean there've been others?!"

"Yes, quite a few, actually. I'm bored here, all the time looking after Andrew. I need excitement and you're always busy."

"Busy earning money to keep us solvent!"

Things went from bad to worse, and Jack was in despair. He couldn't believe that his beautiful wife, whom he loved dearly, could cheat on him like this, over and over again. He would often come home and could tell that she had picked somebody up.

Jack quickly realized that there was a mental health problem with Myra, and he tried to persuade her to seek help. She would have none of it.

When the war ended, Jack said he was going to see if he could manage to buy a house back home in Manchester.

"I don't want to live in Manchester," declared Myra.

"I don't think you have a say, considering how you've let me down! My concern is that Andrew will have a safe environment to be brought up in. I have relatives there who can help out. You can get a job, to give you something to occupy yourself; a fresh start in a new place might stop all this promiscuous behaviour."

"Good, I might find some nice new studs in Manchester!"

One day, in early 1947, Jack came back from ambulance duty as white as a sheet.

"What's the matter? You look as if you've seen a ghost."

"I had a phone call from our family solicitor before I left: my dad has died.

"That means we're both orphans."

"I've been given leave to go home and sort things out: arrange the funeral, etc. You'll have to stay here with Andrew."

"Well, if it's convenient, can I at least come to the funeral?"

"We'll see."

Jack left for Manchester and booked into the same guest house he and Myra had stayed at, then went to the nursing home.

The matron assured him that Harry had died peacefully, and showed Jack into the chapel where his body was. The coffin lid was open; his dad looked happy, relaxed and peaceful, as if the strains of his illness had just faded away. She left him for a while, and asked him to visit her office when he was ready.

He knew that the home had an arrangement with a local undertaker, so it was just a matter of settling up with the home, removing Harry's personal items and contacting their vicar to arrange a service in St. John's, where the family had worshipped all their lives. He said a prayer, kissed his father on the forehead and made the sign of the cross, before going to the matron's office.

"Thank you for all you have done, Matron. I know how well you have all really looked after him here."

"He was a lovely man and we all loved him. We shall miss him greatly."

"I need to make an appointment to see our solicitor, then I can settle up with you, whatever the balance is."

"It's not much, Jack; your father had an arrangement with the bank. A banker's draft ensured the money came in regularly, with no problems at all."

"Oh, okay; that's fine, then. I'll settle up when I know the score."

"I have a few important documents and items here, which he asked me to keep safe for him, in the event of his death: an old passport, an insurance policy, his watch and a cheque book, which will tell you the name of the bank and his account number, etc. Also, do you want me to take his wedding ring off, so you can keep it?"

"Yes, please. I'd like to wear it myself, if it fits."

"Also, do you want to take his clothes, or shall I distribute them amongst some of our other gentlemen here?"

"Oh, yes, please; Dad would like that."

"We always wait a good while after the funeral, and are very discreet in the way we pass them on."

"I'm sure."

"So, I'll just wait to hear from you about the funeral. I know I will be attending, and one or two other staff members who may be available. We all thought the world of your father."

"Thank you, Matron."

"Best wishes, Jack. See you soon."

"'Bye."

Jack was astonished that his father had made an arrangement with his bank; he didn't think his dad had any financial instinct at all! He knew that Harry had inherited some money from his late wife Rebecca's family in Berlin, but he didn't know how much.

When he got back to the hotel, he telephoned the vicar.

"Father Brian? It's me: Jack Blake. My dad has died."

"Oh, Jack, I'm so sorry! One of my congregation told me this morning, at our weekday Mass. How are you coping?"

"Well, I'm okay, I suppose. I need to arrange a funeral with you."

"Yes, of course. Come by tomorrow morning and we'll sort it out."

"Okay, thanks."

Next, Jack rang the family solicitor and arranged to meet him, after seeing the vicar. Then, he rang Myra and gave her an update; he said that he would be home as soon as possible.

The next morning, he had a long chat with Father Brian, who was surprised to learn that Jack had married.

"A wartime bride, eh, Jack?"

"Well, we couldn't wait!"

The funeral was arranged for the Friday of the following week. Hymns and readings were chosen, and Father Brian said that he would do the eulogy, as Jack didn't feel up to it.

He left the vicarage and popped into a local restaurant for lunch. Although the war was over, there was still rationing, so the menu was meagre. Still, he enjoyed his baked potato with baked beans.

Soon, it was time to visit the solicitor, so he made his way to the Piccadilly area of Manchester and found the office.

"Come in, Jack. Take a seat," said the solicitor, warmly. "I'm so sorry about your dad. He was a fine man."

"Thank you. I've brought his cheque book, which should help you to trace his bank account. I'm the only heir, so when it's all settled I need to pay the balance at the nursing home."

The solicitor looked at him for a moment, before speaking.

"Jack, you do know your father inherited money from his late wife's family in Berlin, don't you?"

"Yes, I'm just hoping there's enough to pay the home and funeral expenses. And yours, of course!"

Silence followed.

The solicitor looked at him for a long time, his expression a mixture of surprise and playful knowing, before he spoke again:

"Your father didn't want you to know how much it was, because he was highly embarrassed about the amount. Especially considering the circumstances."

"What do you mean?"

"It was a fortune, Jack. Five million pounds!"

Jack's jaw dropped. His voice finally came out, raspily. "What?! There's some mistake, surely."

"No mistake." The solicitor was smiling now, delighted to impart the welcome surprise. "Your late grandmother hailed from a wealthy family of jewellers, in Berlin. The other members of the family must have all died in the war, and in the will it said that, in the case of no survivors, the fortune was to go to Rebecca or her husband."

"Goodness! I'm stunned," managed a perplexed Jack. "He kept that quiet."

"I know this is a shock, but he took me into his confidence. Because of his illness, he couldn't really be bothered about the money, as long as there was enough to pay the nursing home. In fact, there was more than enough in his own investments, without having to touch that. He said it would be a wonderful surprise for you, and would give new life opportunities to you and your lovely new wife."

Lovely new wife! Perhaps this would bring her to her senses – and help relieve the boredom she claimed to be subjected to.

"Jack?"

"Sorry, I was just pondering on what to do with so much money! I can't conceive of keeping it all for myself. Having lived through the war and seen so much hardship – people's lives ruined, homes destroyed… – it seems immoral to spend all that on ourselves. I want to do some good with it."

"Well, once everything is sorted, you will have plenty of time to talk things through with your wife and do whatever you want to."

Jack returned to the guest house.

After the evening meal, he went out to find a telephone box. He rang Myra's brother, Joe.

"Hello, Joe, it's Jack."

"Oh, Jack, I'm so sorry to hear about your dad. How are you doing?"

"I'm shocked – for more reasons than one! I'm in Manchester. I thought I would take a detour to London, to see you and Clare, before returning to Cardiff. I need to talk to you."

"That's no problem, Jack. I hope everything's okay."

"Can I travel down tomorrow?"

"Yes, no problem. See you then. Are you alright?"

"Sort of. I'll explain everything tomorrow; can't do it over the phone."

"Okay, take care."

Joe put the phone down and turned to Clare. "Gosh, it sounds as if he's taken it really badly. There's something not right, I can tell."

"Are you sure?"

"Yes, he doesn't sound himself. He's coming here first, before going home to Myra."

"Well, then we'll know tomorrow."

Chapter 26

1966

SWITZERLAND

GEORGE STANHOPE HAD located the rest of the Goldberg estate: it was indeed in the Bank Lombard Odier.

He, Aaron and Jack travelled to Switzerland, taking all the necessary documentation with them. That took more than one meeting with the bank manager, his assistant and one or two clerks; Aaron only had a visa allowing him to stay in Britain! His birth certificate had been stolen by the Russian officer who had thrust him into further captivity. Ultimately, it was the documents from the Russian embassy, the Jewish Restitutional Office in Berlin, Herr Grüber's letter and the Home Secretary's correspondence which did the trick, together with Rebecca's will.

Eventually, arrangements were made to transfer the money to a new account in London, in Aaron's name. It amounted to five million pounds. Aaron was staggered.

They had booked into a hotel and discussed the future over dinner.

"Well, Aaron, you are officially a multi-millionaire!" said George. "When we have sorted out the charity, you will have an enormous fortune at your disposal."

"I've been thinking a lot about that. I don't want to disband the charity; it doesn't seem right to me. It's the Nazis' fault that this money did not stay in my family's possession, not yours. The fact that the money has been put to such good use, my father would be so pleased about: to see the family fortune used in this wonderful way. There's absolutely no point in destroying a good thing. Besides, can you imagine the press? They would go to town, exposing me for destroying such a worthwhile charity."

"I can see that, Aaron, but the money is rightfully yours," said Jack.

"I know, but it's an obscene amount of money for one person to own. My father never told us how much money the business was worth; all he ever told us was that he only ever used the interest to give above-average wages to his employees, together with bonuses for Christmas, Easter vacations, and staff outings and parties. He also gave regularly to charities. All of this was before the Nazis came to power, of course. In fact, once he could see the way things were going, he transferred the money to Switzerland.

"I've decided that, to make it work, you can put me on the charity's board of trustees. My presence there and the Goldberg name listed will give legal consent to its existence as a charity, and its continuing work. Then, I want to set up another charity of my own with this five million, to help people who have been affected by war and displacement: refugees, etc."

"Are you sure?" said George.

"Absolutely! I will, however, need to buy a house and a car out of some of the money; I need to become a British citizen. There's so much to do, and there's no life for me in Germany now. If it hadn't been divided, and my old home was not in the Soviet sector, then I may have been able to find old family friends and build a new life. But, apart from Herr Grüber – who is quite old now – I don't know anyone there. I will have nothing in common with people who have been indoctrinated by communist ideals."

"Well, we can do everything possible to help you. A phone call to the Home Office is top of the list, to get you citizenship. Then, we can go house hunting," said Jack.

Jack once more rang the Home Office and spoke to his contact there, who put him in touch with the British Jewish Refugee Committee, which was set up during the war, to help Jews fleeing the Nazi terror. The regulations set up by this committee, with government approval, declared that Aaron would need to live and work in Britain for five years to receive automatic citizenship.

With this knowledge, upon their return Jack, Andrew and Aaron set out house hunting. Obviously money was no problem, and Aaron wanted to be near Andrew and Jack, so a modern apartment in

Knightsbridge was settled upon. It was palatial, and within walking distance of Andrew's boutique; a short drive away was Jack's own palace.

With help from the family solicitor, Jack and George Stanhope set up the Goldberg Trust for Displaced People. Almost immediately Aaron found himself helping fellow Jews, who had fled Europe during the war and lost everything; they were now struggling to recover their property in the lands they had escaped from. It also extended to other Europeans, who had come to Britain for refuge during the war. Aaron's real purpose, though, was to investigate prisoners in the Gulag system who, like himself, had been robbed of their lives, property, dignity and, in many cases, their health.

His story soon hit the headlines, which gave more credence to the Blake Charity Foundation. The shame of his story embarrassed the Russian embassy and, in spite of the Cold War, they offered their help. They even allowed him to visit the embassy from time to time, and make contact with the Administrative Board of the Gulag system.

Pressure was put on the authorities to consider that their methods of arrest and interrogation should be more humane. It was also pointed out that, although they were not a democracy, they might like to think about the western idea that one is innocent until proven guilty! This was asking a lot but, because of the embarrassing publicity, the authorities cooperated; Aaron had appeared on various television programmes, relating his life story. Newspapers galore wanted to feature him, and he soon had celebrity status – this ensured an investigation into Benjamin's false arrest.

It took no time at all to locate Benjamin, who was at the camp where Aaron had been incarcerated, and they were able to successfully get him released.

The charity paid for Benjamin's travel documents and Aaron went to Moscow to meet him, at the same hotel where Jack and Andrew had met Aaron.

"Benjamin!" he shouted, upon sighting his friend. "Benjamin! Over here!"

Benjamin looked across the road and saw Aaron, standing outside the Hotel International. He hurried across the road and they embraced. Benjamin then burst into tears.

Eventually, when he had composed himself, he said: "Oh, Aaron, I can't believe you've been able to get me out of that place! I thought I was going to be there for the rest of my life."

"Well, my friend, it was easy. Once they traced the person who stole your identity, and found him to be a Nazi, guilty of war crimes, they couldn't get you out of there quickly enough, I can tell you!"

"Thank you, thank you, thank you, my friend!" said Benjamin. He started crying again.

Aaron said: "We can't have you crying in the middle of the street. We might get arrested again!"

"I'm sorry. I just can't believe this is happening."

"I know. I felt the same when Jack and Andrew came to collect me."

"Who are they?"

"I'll give you an update when we are inside the hotel, and you are a bit more settled. But be sure of this: I'm going to make it my lifelong mission to expose that Gulag system and help destroy it."

"Well, I'll help you, mate – I really will!"

"Come on, let's get you inside. I've booked a room for you, and we need to get you some decent clothes and things."

"I've got nothing!"

"Don't worry; money is no object. I'll explain everything; just follow me and let me do the talking."

They went into the hotel, and for Aaron it was a case of déjà vu. He took great delight in ordering drinks and nibbles, while they chatted about some of the other inmates in their work gang.

Aaron realized that it was going to be more difficult to release some of them, as they were Russian and not German or Polish. It may not be possible at all, in fact, if there was no connection to Nazism.

He told Benjamin all that had happened to him, his newfound family, the reclaimed Goldberg fortune, Myra and José's remarkable story and the trust he had set up. Benjamin was astonished.

After they had enjoyed some champagne and canapés, Aaron

said: "Come on, mate, it's time to go shopping."

He took Benjamin to the same stores that Andrew had taken him into, previously. Later, they returned to the hotel and Aaron settled Benjamin in his room. He explained that he would call in later, to go for dinner in the dining hall. Aaron knew exactly how Benjamin would be feeling, and couldn't help grinning at his awed expressions.

"What's so funny?" said Benjamin. "I know: I look a wreck!"

"Nothing is funny. I'm just amused because all of this reminds me of when Andrew and Jack met me here: it's a repeat of the whole situation! Déjà vu! How drastically my life has changed since then, Benjy! The same will happen for you, if you're willing to join me in my new job, and let me help you make a new life for yourself."

"Are you sure you want me to work for you? I'm not really skilled at anything, other than hard labour. The Nazis and Soviets stole my life, remember? Just like you."

"Absolutely! Together we can provide the compassion needed to deal with some of the people who come to us for help. You wouldn't believe the cases we've dealt with already, since I set up the charity."

"Thank you, Aaron! You're all I have. All of my family perished in Treblinka, like yours did in Auschwitz."

"Well, tomorrow we fly to London. I'm going to open a bank account for you and put some money in it. You can live with me until we find a suitable home for you and, under the charities' constitution, we'll agree upon a suitable wage for you. Then, you can begin a new life!"

"Oh, goodness, I can't believe it!"

"You will, my friend, you will. Trust me."

Aaron took great delight in escorting Benjamin to the restaurant later, after he had showered and changed into his new clothes. Just like he had been, Benjamin was stunned by everything he saw: the décor, the food, the wine…!

"This is a little bit different to Siberia! I can't believe we're in the same country!" said Benjamin.

"I know. Such hypocrisy, really. All of this is to impress foreigners, even though they don't really want many here. The ordinary Soviet citizen lives in very humble surroundings; they all look like concrete blocks. Andrew says they remind him of a prison."

"Still, even they must be better than the rat-infested huts in the death camps!" said Benjamin.

Benjamin took a long time to get to sleep that night. His emotions were all mixed up. He was relieved to be free, and excited about the future, but also a little nervous. Overall, though, he was sad that his wonderful family couldn't share all of this with him – they had met a terrible end.

The next day they travelled to London.

Andrew met them at the airport and took them to Aaron's apartment.

After settling in, everything was quickly set into motion for a bewildered but very happy Benjamin, with the help of Jack and Andrew. He was now an employee of the Goldberg Trust.

He stayed with Aaron until they were able to buy a suitable apartment. Eventually, though, he was well set up, and found himself settling into his new life, with the help of his newfound family. Very well set up, indeed.

Chapter 27

1966

SAN CAYETANO, SPAIN

"WILL YOU MARRY me, Alma?" said José.

Silence...

"Well?"

"Yes, absolutely! But we'll have to have Papá's permission. You know how things are here."

"Well, I think he likes me. I'll ask him on Sunday, when I come for another one of your epic lunches, okay?"

"Yes, but just wait until we're having dessert and he's had a good couple of glasses of rioja!"

They both laughed.

José returned home and told Antonio, who by now had already met Alma. He had approved of her a long time ago, and was secretly hoping that they would become an item. He couldn't thank Diego enough, for looking out for his boy and introducing him to Alma.

"It's all down to Alma's father now, Papá!"

"Well, Mateo is a bit of an old goat, but I get along alright with him, because of the business. Don't worry about it, son; he wouldn't have allowed you to go there for Sunday lunches all of these months if he didn't like you, or have an idea of what is going on between you two."

"If he gives his consent, I want to take her to London to meet the rest of the family. And I want you to come, as well!"

Silence...

"Well?"

"Okay, son, I'll come. It will be good to see your home, even though it was Myra's."

"Well, just remember it's Jack's, really; he bought it. In fact, all traces of her have been removed; Andrew gave everything to his father's charity. When the charity begins to set homeless people up in new accommodation, they are always grateful for furniture, etc. I told Andrew that some things could stay, but he would have none of it; everything had to go! It was as much as he could do to enter the house, even though he had been brought up there! It doesn't bother me because I never knew her, and have never lived in that house like Andrew did," said José.

"Well, it's going to work out well, because old Mateo will see that I'm acting as a chaperone. He would never let you take her there on your own. You realize that, don't you?"

"Yes, I hadn't thought about that. Although, I could have put her up in a hotel."

"Yes, but would he believe that?" said Antonio. They both laughed.

"I have a vision of the whole family travelling to London," said José. "Half the population of San Cayetano would be missing!"

They both laughed again.

Sunday couldn't come quickly enough for José. When it did, he was as nervous as a kitten.

Antonio couldn't help having a giggle. "Come on, son; it'll be fine. Just wait until he says yes before telling him you're absconding with her to London!" He laughed.

"Papá, that's not funny!"

"I'm only teasing. Just be sure to tell him I'm coming with you, for goodness' sake!"

Lunch at the villa in San Cayetano extended into early evening, as usual; desserts were served about six p.m.!

After copious amounts of vino, José realized that if he left it any later Mateo would be blotto, and not able to make a reasoned approval of his desire to marry Alma. So, he caught Alma's eye, and she banged the table with her spoon.

"Papá, José has something to say."

Her mother Sonia grinned and gave Alma a knowing look, while her sisters suppressed giggles. The female contingent of the family had already discussed the proposition and obviously approved. It was all down to Mateo now.

"What is it you have to say, my boy?"

"I want your permission to marry Alma, señor."

Silence...

José froze. The silence seemed like an eternity.

Then, Mateo laughed loudly and banged his wine glass on the table.

"About time, José! Do you think I'm stupid? I've seen the way you two look at each other; I thought you'd never ask! More vino, Sonia; it's time to celebrate!"

"Do you really think you should have any more, Mateo?" said Sonia.

"Yes, it's time to celebrate! Salud!"

Everyone sighed with relief – not least José.

So, as the so-called Sunday lunch merged with the evening meal, Mateo phoned Antonio and demanded he drive up to join them. Antonio knew not to argue with Mateo and got into his car quickly, delighted that things had gone well.

When Antonio arrived, a glass of vino was thrust into his hands; he was embraced by all and treated like a lord. The evening continued with toasts to the happy couple and family stories. Fortunately, everyone knew José's sad story.

Soon, Mateo was having to hold back his verbal abuse of Franco and his regime.

"Shush, Papá; you don't know who's on the street listening!" said Alma. "Sound carries when we're outdoors like this!"

"It's time this country became a democracy! It's a disgrace that we are held back by Franco and his Church!"

"Don't let Father Pedro hear you talk like that, or the Guardia Civil will be knocking at the door! Goodness knows what will become of you then! What will become of us all!" said Sonia.

Antonio was the one who broached the subject of José taking Alma to London, to meet his stepbrother and the rest of the family. He could see that the day had gone well, so he risked mentioning it. He explained that, because of José's lack of a normal family upbringing, and because of Myra's behaviour, he felt it was important for José to show off his bride-to-be to the London contingent.

Fortunately, Mateo agreed. For one horrible moment, Antonio and José thought that he was going to come with them! But Mateo was pleased that Antonio would act as a chaperone, and instead insisted that he and Sonia pay for the flights.

By midnight, it was obvious that neither José nor Antonio could drive home after all the wine which had been drunk, so they were shown to guest rooms in the palatial villa.

The next morning, there were a few delays with the fruit and vegetables being prepared at the finca, and with the produce being collected by Antonio and his drivers for distribution. Needless to say, hangovers were in abundance.

When they had all sobered up, they went to visit Father Pedro. Mateo, Sonia, José, Alma and Antonio settled themselves in the presbytery, which was adjoined to the church in San Cayetano. A date was fixed for August 4th. Father Pedro encouraged this date, as it would be in the period of the fiesta for the village, and would be seen as a wonderful, happy event for the villagers, as they approached the Feast Day of San Cayetano, on 7th August. The family were delighted.

Mateo insisted that the London family members should come. Between his villa and the spare accommodation at the finca, there would be room for them all to stay, and make for a wonderful occasion.

A few days later, with the capable Julio in charge of the business, Antonio, José and Alma made their way to Alicante, to fly to Heathrow. Mateo drove them there, as the train service from Balsicas was not reliable. Farewells were exchanged and Mateo wished them well.

"Your Papá is quite a character, Alma," said Antonio, after Mateo had driven away.

"I know! For one horrible moment, I thought he and Mama were going to come with us! I think that would have been too much for your British family, José!"

"Oh, they'd have coped. They are an extremely versatile family, after all they've been through. I'm sure you'll love them, and I know they'll love you!"

They landed at Heathrow, and Jack was there to pick them up and take them to José's home. Jack welcomed Alma and said that he had arranged a family party that night at his home, to greet her.

After he dropped them off at the house, Antonio and Alma made themselves comfortable.

"So, this is where she lived?"

"Yes, Papá. But don't worry; there's no trace of her here now. Nothing to bring back those horrendous memories."

"I know, son. But to think that she lived here in style yet planned your abortion! I can't believe it!"

Alma hugged him and said: "Papá… Can I call you that?"

"Yes, of course, cariño; August isn't far away. How delightful to have a daughter!"

She hugged him tighter and continued: "Well, with José's extended family here in London, and my tribe in San Cayetano, we're going to make one big, happy family, which is going to more than make up for the past. And when our little niños come along, that will be the cream on the top."

They all laughed, as Alma went to make coffee.

Later, they popped out to a restaurant for a light lunch. Jack warned them that Madge, his superb housekeeper, was quite good at serving up foreign cuisine, and told them all about Aaron's first night. She had been studying the art of Spanish tapas for some time, and they were in for a feast, so: "For goodness' sake, don't have too much for lunch!"

After a light lunch, they met up again and drove to Jack's home in Knightsbridge.

Antonio was astonished at the house and grounds, while Alma took it all in her stride, having come from a huge villa in Spain. The only thing missing for her was the sun!

"Are the skies always blanketed in cloud, like this?" said Alma.

"We do get sun sometimes, but plenty of rain as well. Just be glad it's dry," said Jack.

Jack introduced Alma to Joe and Clare, Andrew, Aaron and Benjamin. Although Benjamin wasn't really family, the others had grown so fond of him that they thought of him as one of their own, and included him in everything.

As promised, Madge had prepared a tapas feast!

There was chorizo in red wine, various tortillas, patatas bravas, prawns in garlic oil, ham croquettes, fried battered squid, a board of serrano ham with cheese and bread, grilled octopus, anchovies in vinegar, red peppers stuffed with tuna and rice, and smoked salmon, together with green salad, Murcian salad and various crisps of differing flavours. José, Alma and Antonio couldn't believe their eyes.

"Can I take Madge back home with me?" said Alma. "Mama would be in Heaven!"

"Sorry, Alma, she's mine!" said Jack. They all laughed.

Then José spoke: "Well, I just want to thank you all for your kindness in welcoming Alma and my father. It is a further gesture of the wonderful love and care you have shown to me since I met you all. Let's raise our glasses to family."

"Salud! To family!" they all shouted.

"Now another toast is required."

They all looked at one another.

José continued: "Alma and I are to be married on the fourth of August in her village church, and you are all welcome. Please raise your glasses to my wonderful bride to be, Alma!"

"Oh, that's wonderful news!" said Jack.

"Salud, Alma!" they all shouted.

Jack dragged Madge in from the kitchen, which gave José an opportunity to thank her and thrust a glass into her hand. There were kisses and hugs all around. Champagne was opened, the rioja flowed and everyone got to know Alma and Antonio, as they ate the wonderful tapas.

Joe, Clare and Antonio reminisced about the time he had turned up at the villa in Spain. Together with Jack, they chatted about Myra. Jack was able to assure Antonio that they all now felt sorry for her untimely death and her mental health problems. Antonio said that, although he had lost years of José's life, everything now was more than making up for it. He hoped that they would all come to the wedding in San Cayetano.

"Wild horses will not keep us away!" said Jack.

Andrew said: "Why don't we have an engagement party, at the villa in Santiago?"

"That sounds great," said José. "However, you'll have to pass it by Mateo, Alma's father. He's quite the patriarch. I wouldn't be surprised if he wasn't a toreador in his younger days!"

They all laughed. Alma came along and, giggling along, said: "Are you making fun of my papá?"

"No, not really," said José.

He told her about Andrew's idea of an engagement party, in the villa at Santiago.

"That sounds great! It will bring a real Spanish connection to us all, as a family. Don't worry about Papá; Mama will sort him out. His bark is worse than his bite!"

They all laughed again.

Chapter 28

1947

LONDON

"JACK! IT'S GOOD to see you, but not in these circumstances, I'm sure."

"Oh, Joe, I'm so confused and upset. I need to talk to you and Clare, before I return to Cardiff."

"Yes, of course, Jack. You worried me a little on the phone yesterday."

"I know. I'm distressed."

"I'll get Clare and she can make us coffee."

While Clare was making the coffee, Jack told Joe about all the funeral arrangements, the wonderful care his dad had received at the nursing home, the matron's kindness and the staff's desire to attend the funeral.

Then, when Clare came in and poured coffee, Jack gave them the rest of his news. He started first with Myra's adultery and her change of behaviour, so out of keeping with the girl he'd fallen madly in love with and married.

"Oh, my goodness, Jack," said Clare. "I'm so sorry!"

"She was always full of nonsense and wickedness, but that was Myra: always getting me into trouble with Mam and Dad. But this… it's a shocker," said Joe.

"There's a hormonal problem after the birth, you take it from me," said Clare.

"I've tried to encourage her to get help, but she won't hear of it."

"Perhaps I can talk to her," said Clare.

"Yes, maybe that would help, Clare. But, be careful; she's like a fiery tiger sometimes! My other news is even more of a shocker, but very different!"

He then told them about his inheritance. They were stunned, and speechless for a moment.

"I can't think of keeping all this money for myself; I feel I want to do some good with it. After all, I've grown up not knowing it was there, anyway."

"Well, that's up to you, Jack," said Joe. "I can see how you feel."

"Dad never touched this money from my grandmother's estate. He had money of his own, which will pay for the funeral with plenty left over," said Jack.

Clare looked at him and said: "Well, whatever good you do, keep something for yourself. Make a new life after this dreadful war. This might change Myra for the better – you never know."

"I admire you, Jack, for not leaving Myra after all the men she's had," said Joe.

"I still love her, Joe. And then there's Andrew, the light of my life."

Clare started crying and Joe held her tight. Jack was holding back the tears, also.

Clare rustled up some lunch, which they ate in silence, pondering this change of events.

"I did think we could move to Manchester but, on reflection, now that money is no problem, I think London would be better, as we can be near you."

"That's great, Jack! We can see more of Andrew then, and help out with babysitting."

After further chats about the future, and Myra's problems, Jack made his farewells and returned to Cardiff.

He wondered if he would find another boy in the prefab with Myra.

Fortunately, she was alone, with Andrew sleeping in his cot.

"Hi, how did things go?" she asked.

"I've got news."

"Oh. I expect you've seen a solicitor, have you, and will be leaving me and Andrew?"

"No, Myra, I'm not leaving. I still love you and Andrew is my son; I can't abandon him!"

Silence…

"What's the news, then?"

"I have seen the family solicitor, but it seems that Dad has left me some money: more than five million pounds!"

"What?!"

"Yes, he inherited it from my grandmother, Rebecca, who hailed from a wealthy family of jewellers in Berlin."

"My god, Jack, that's wonderful! We're millionaires!"

"Yes, it's going to change our lives considerably. I think perhaps London would be a better place to move to than Manchester, so we can be near Joe and Clare."

Myra dashed over to Jack, embraced him, showered him with kissed and said: "Oh, Jack, that's great! It will be a new start for us, and Andrew won't want for anything. I'm so excited."

"Well, after the funeral Joe and Clare said we can stay with them, to do some house hunting!"

"Great, I can't wait! This is fantastic!" said Myra.

Jack was a little taken aback that there seemed to be no compassion for her bereaved husband in Myra's reaction. However, he had high hopes that things might right themselves. They hadn't slept together for a long time because of her behaviour, but in time the hurt might heal.

The funeral was conducted with great dignity by Father Brian. Many of the congregation had turned up, because they remembered Harold with affection, and Jack had been a chorister and server at the church, until he joined the Ambulance Service and moved to Cardiff. The interment took place in the church grounds, where Harry was buried with his beloved Rebecca who, although Jewish, had become an Anglican many years before.

After the service, they went to a nearby hotel for refreshments, which Jack had previously arranged. There they met many of Harry's friends, and some distant relatives who Jack didn't really know. Needless to say there was no one from Berlin. Matron was also there, with two members of staff, and Jack was so touched that they had made the effort to come.

Once everything was settled, the family made the journey to London, to stay with Joe and Clare, and begin house hunting.

When they had unpacked and settled in, Clare made a wonderful supper of lasagne, roasted vegetables and salad. They enjoyed some wine and relaxed.

The next day, Clare was happy to babysit Andrew, while Joe took Jack and Myra out to start looking for suitable houses. It was exhausting but quite exciting, with money being no problem.

They settled on a four-bedroomed house in fashionable Knightsbridge, and Myra was delighted. She couldn't wait to move in. They decided to buy new furniture, as everything she had in the prefab was second-hand and nothing matched.

"Oh, Jack, this is like a dream. I can't believe it's happening!"

Still no concern for a bereaved husband!

Clare wanted to speak to Myra privately about the way things were, but Joe had warned her that now was not the right time.

"Wait until they've moved here and then, with Jack's permission, we can broach the subject. In any case, perhaps Jack is right: this change of circumstances may alter things."

"Yes, let's hope so; funnier things have happened. In any case, that's better, because we don't want a big scene now, just after the funeral."

A couple of weeks later, when all was signed and contracts exchanged, they came again to stay with Joe and Clare. This time it was to buy furniture and deal with the frustration of waiting for deliveries.

Jack had resigned from the Ambulance Service and was taking the time to think things through. He didn't really need to work, being a millionaire, but wanted to sort things out as soon as possible.

Eventually, all was settled: the beautiful house was furnished with all the latest designs and Myra was ecstatic.

"Oh, Jack, this is fabulous! I can't believe how lucky we've been!"

"Well, yes. It's all down to my dad; I had no idea he'd inherited so much from my gran."

"We must raise a glass to Rebecca," said Myra.

"Well, Dad had some money of his own, besides this fortune. I thought I'd buy a holiday home in Spain."

"Oh, that's fantastic, Jack; how wonderful! Andrew will grow up experiencing holidays in Spain."

As soon as all the furniture had been delivered and services connected, they moved in and settled quite quickly.

Clare and Joe came around for a little housewarming party and everything seemed settled… for a while.

Very soon, they booked a holiday in Spain.

They both agreed that they wanted a little bit of "real" Spain when it came to purchasing a property; they didn't want to be stuck in some tourist trap, where they would likely meet people they knew. So, the travel agent suggested a new developing area call the Mar Menor. They took his advice and found themselves holidaying on what was known as the Manga Strip. It was okay, but they had to take a ferry to get to the mainland, or drive miles along the strip, which was a bit tedious – though they did enjoy the nightlife in all the bars and restaurants.

On the mainland, they were very taken with the seaside resort of Santiago de la Ribera. They searched properties for sale, many of which were delightful, and couldn't believe how cheap they were! However, they always came back to one particular property, which they both felt drawn to: a villa on the seafront. It was very grand, and just across the road from the beach.

"I know it's rather big," said Jack, "but we can make use of it with all of the family; your brother and Clare can come out. We'll have a ball!"

"Let's find the estate agent and have a look inside," said Myra, excitedly.

The estate agent was just around the corner on the main street, and they walked to the office to express their interest. One of the members of staff had reasonably good English, so they were able to ask questions about the villa on the seafront. The agent seemed very pleased, and said that he could take them there straight away, as he was not too busy. He brought along the young man with good English, leaving the shop in the hands of another member of staff, to take them to the villa on the seafront.

The English-speaking boy told them that it had belonged to a family in Madrid, but with most of the family killed in the Spanish civil war, the remaining family couldn't really afford to keep it anymore, and wanted the money out of it.

The grounds around the villa were very well kept and provided good outside space, but the inside was stunning. Myra loved the spacious rooms and the beautiful Spanish furniture. The view over the beach was wonderful; they could see right over to the Manga Strip, where they were staying. The building was in such good condition, it didn't take long for them to agree on a price; Jack couldn't believe how cheap such a magnificent property was.

They were taken to a solicitor and all the necessary arrangements were made. It would take a few months, but eventually they would all be able to have a family holiday together, in sunny Spain.

After their holiday, Jack and Myra returned to London and told Joe and Clare all about the villa. They agreed that, once things were settled, they would have a holiday together on the seafront. Myra assured Joe and Clare that they would love the place.

"It's so unspoiled," said Myra; "not a tourist in sight."

During the ensuing months, Jack felt that things were almost back to normal between him and Myra. He'd always found it easy to forgive and, because he loved Myra and Andrew so much, it came easily to him. He wondered if her behaviour might have been a post-natal thing. They enjoyed their new luxury home, and couldn't wait to make their first visit to the villa in Spain.

As soon as things were settled and the villa purchased, they flew to Spain.

Myra was happy to keep most of the furniture; it was typically Spanish and they both loved it. There were just a few items to purchase, and of course bedding, crockery, cutlery and all the necessary things to make it a home. They enjoyed doing this together on the first few days.

Maybe it was the sunshine, the romantic environment of a villa on the seafront, or more likely Jack's plans to create a charity out of his inheritance, which made Myra take a turn for the worse…

On their holiday, they argued most of the time about why he would want to use that money for other than themselves!

"What about Andrew?" shouted Myra.

"Well, the charity is going to run itself, and the interest will pay the wages of any staff. I want to do something good with it. It's a colossal amount of money, which we didn't know we were going to have, anyway."

Myra sulked and the holiday was ruined.

She would go off on her own to sunbathe. Jack was suspicious one day, when he saw her walking off the beach with a young man. Where was she going?

He quickly put Andrew in the pram and left the villa to follow her. They walked into the side-streets of the little town and Jack kept his distance. Eventually, he saw her going into a house with the boy.

He made his way back to the villa and settled Andrew. Then, he contacted the flight company and explained that something had cropped up; he needed to bring forward his flight, to the nearest date possible. This took some time and cost quite a lot, but Jack was determined he wasn't going to stay for a full fortnight, putting up with her behaviour.

When she returned much later, he said: "Enjoy yourself, did you? You'll be cradle-snatching next! He looked a lot younger than you, Myra!"

"You bastard! You followed me!"

"It's not difficult to see what's going on when the villa is practically on the beach!"

"I hate you!"

"By the way, I've brought forward our flights; we're returning to London the day after tomorrow."

"What? You sod! Well, I'm not coming."

"Fine. Andrew and I will return, and you can fend for yourself in a foreign country with no money and no Spanish. I wish you well with that."

She went upstairs and slammed the bedroom door shut.

That night, Jack slept in one of the spare rooms. Well, sleep didn't actually come; he was too depressed. He couldn't wait to get back home.

He was more determined than ever now to set up the charity. He felt he wanted to do something for homeless people. He'd seen so many lose their homes during the war, while he had been so fortunate. Then, to have his father's inheritance, their lives changed dramatically and a luxury home in London and Spain, he felt that he needed to give something back. If Myra was so selfish that she couldn't come on board with him, then so be it.

He thought back to her behaviour in Cardiff and quickly realized that she had a mental health problem. If she didn't show such love and affection toward Andrew, he would be worried for the child's safety. It was like she had a dual personality: she was the loving, doting mother to Andrew, but acted like a whore on the streets of Cardiff – and, it seemed, Spain as well. It sickened him. What would she be like in London?! Thank goodness they would have Joe and Clare nearby, he thought.

Two days later, a taxi picked them up for the journey to Alicante, where they boarded a flight to London. Myra didn't open her mouth once, other than to coo Andrew and whisper sweet things to him.

They landed at Heathrow and took a taxi home.

The next day, Jack went to the solicitor and began the process of setting up the Blake Charity Foundation.

When he returned home, he told Myra what he had done. It would be run by himself and an assistant to start with; if things worked out well, it could expand with more staff. The interest on the initial investment would pay for the staff and the running of the charity. It was all being dealt with by the family solicitor, while media attention helped build his profile.

"Well, you can piss off from here; I don't want you around!" shouted Myra. "What a waste of time and money: helping dropouts! You must be mad!"

"This is my house, bought out of my father's inheritance. You're the one who can piss off!"

"I expect you're having it off with all those dropouts!"

"Only your disgusting mind could think of such a thing. I'll tell you what, though: you can throw me out! You can have the house – not for you, though; for Andrew. I'll buy another house somewhere else, but I want access to Andrew; I'm his father and I want to be part of his life."

"What's keeping you, sunshine? Get packing and piss off!"

Jack telephoned Joe and Clare, and asked if he could stay there for a day or two, while he sorted himself out. They were disgusted with Myra and welcomed Jack. They had plenty of space and told him to take as long as he needed.

It didn't take him long to purchase a new property, as money was no object. He made arrangements with the solicitor to sign the house over to Myra, but was warned that custody of the child would go to Myra, and he would have to fight for access to Andrew.

Within a week or so, Jack moved into a fashionable house in Knightsbridge. It had three bedrooms and what the estate agent called a "granny flat"; Jack jokingly preferred to call it the "west wing". He imagined that, when Andrew was old enough, he would enjoy staying and having his own space – maybe bring friends to stay.

Unfortunately, this would never happen. Custody naturally went to the mother – something Jack had to accept – because she lied her way through a session in the magistrates' court, about Jack's alleged affairs and the fact that he had walked out and deserted her. He didn't stand a chance. As Andrew grew up, she poisoned him against Jack, so much that the boy didn't want to have anything to do with him.

Joe and Clare comforted Jack through all of this, and tried to make Myra see reason, but she was too busy picking up young men, leaving Andrew either in the care of her friends, or with Joe and Clare.

"Mam would be disgusted with you, Myra!" Joe condemned her. "She didn't bring you up to behave like this. She gave us all a good grounding."

"Don't bring her into this! It's my life and I'll live it the way I want to. You're just as bad as that wimp I'm married to!"

Chapter 29

1967

LONDON

"AARON, DO YOU want to come to my staff do at the Criterion next Saturday?" asked Andrew.

"Oh, I don't know. I'm not very good at socializing!"

"It will only be my two assistants, both of whom you know from the shop, and some staff members from other boutiques in Carnaby Street. We all tend to muddle together. It'll be fun!"

"I'll think about it," said Aaron.

"Look, mate, you're a good-looking guy; you'll pick up with a girl in no time. That's just what you need. You've got a new life now and you must make the most of it."

"I'm shy and nervous, Andrew! I've never been with a girl. I was taken to Auschwitz at thirteen – there was no opportunity there for relationships, as you can well imagine. Then, I was carted off to ice-cold Siberia – once again, no chance of a relationship."

"Oh, I'm sorry, Aaron; how insensitive of me. I just didn't think about any of that, and the implications of living in Hell for all those years. Please accept my apologies."

"No worries, Andrew. It'll come right in time. The trouble is I'm thirty-seven now and I've never had sex! I don't think I'd be any good with a girl."

Aaron looked at him in stunned silence, considering his words. Then, he walked over to Aaron and gave him a hug.

"It's alright, mate. It'll come naturally when you're with the right girl. You're not gay, are you?"

"What's that?"

"I mean you're not a homosexual, are you?"

"I don't know what I am, but I certainly don't feel attracted to men! In Auschwitz, some men tried it on with each other, in desperation for human comfort, but when they were caught they were tortured and shot. Some of the S.S. were total hypocrites, because one or two of them were homosexuals; they would take new inmates who hadn't lost their weight or looks, and use them as sex slaves. Then, they would send them to the gas when they were fed up with them, only to select new victims among the steady stream of new arrivals."

"Oh, my god! How disgusting!" said Andrew.

"Fortunately, no-one selected me."

"Well, I was only asking because, if you were gay, there would not be need to worry about it; in February the government passed a new law decriminalizing it, so it is quite legal to have a gay relationship."

"Why do you call it 'gay'? When I was learning English, 'gay' meant light-hearted, carefree, cheerful and merry?"

"It's just an expression, chosen to make a different lifestyle harmlessly acceptable, I suppose; I'm not really sure. Anyway, I'm going to introduce you to some great girls. They will come flocking to you with those looks of yours."

"Do you think so?"

"I know so! This is London in the swinging 'sixties! Don't worry, I'll look after you."

"Okay, then I'll come. But, what about you? Have you got a girlfriend?"

"I've had loads; I just haven't found the right one. I think they were all after my money. At the moment I'm stepping back for a bit. After hearing of my mother's behaviour, I'm a bit sickened, to be honest with you. I just need a bit of time."

"Yes, I see."

"Anyway, great that you're going to come. When we arrive, we'll have something to eat first. It's fashionable to have basket meals these days."

"Basket meals?"

"Yes, maybe chicken and chips in a basket, or fish and chips... whatever."

"You have some funny words and expressions for things which are not in the *Oxford English Dictionary* I use to further my English studies," laughed Aaron.

Andrew laughed, too, and said: "Well, there's a lot more I can teach you. We tend to call girls 'birds'; 'groovy' means 'cool'; something wonderful is 'fab', which is short for fabulous; 'bread' means money; and 'having a gas' means having fun. You'll learn!"

They both laughed before he continued:

"Anyway, after food we go upstairs in the Criterion for a disco."

"Disco?"

"A dance."

Aaron froze. "I can't dance!"

"It's easy."

Andrew put a 45 single of The Beatles' "Day Tripper" on his Dansette record player, and started jigging about.

Aaron laughed his socks off. "You call that dancing?" Continuing to laugh, he thought of the glamorous balls his mother and father went to, before the Nazis seized power; how elegant she looked in her gowns, and how smart his father was in tails.

"Well, I think I can jig like that, if that's what everyone else does," he grinned.

"You'll be fine."

So, Aaron went with Andrew to his boutique's staff party at the Criterion, and indeed met lots of girls. It wasn't just his good looks which attracted them, but the fact that he was something of a celebrity, having told his story to the media. They had enormous respect for him, for setting up a charity with the money.

There was one girl, however, who seemed a cut above all the others. She was intelligent, smartly dressed in a mini-skirt and a tasteful blouse, and seemed genuinely interested in Aaron as a person, rather than a wealthy celebrity. Her name was Gloria, and they hit it off immediately. She was stunning to look at, with a trim figure, golden complexion, blonde hair and blue eyes. For a moment, he could have mistaken her for an Aryan, God forbid! They talked together, danced (or, as Aaron joked, "jigged about") and laughed a lot.

At the end of the evening, she asked if she could see him again. Aaron was a bit taken aback that she should be so forward, but

Andrew had warned him that the swinging 'sixties had changed everything. So, he smiled and said that he would like that very much indeed. They agreed on a dinner date, in a fashionable restaurant in Knightsbridge. They would meet first at the Criterion the following Friday, for a drink, then move on to the Dolce Vita Italian restaurant for dinner.

"Your parents won't mind that you're going out with someone they've never met before, and that I'm Jewish, will they?"

"No, Aaron, they are not prejudiced idiots! Besides, they know Jack and Andrew well, and any friend of theirs will be perfectly acceptable, you'll see," said Gloria.

"Will you be alright in the Criterion on your own, if I'm delayed because of traffic?"

"Don't worry, my dad will be dropping me off. If you're not there, he'll hang around until you come."

"Oh, okay. I'll make sure I'm very early, then," said the now terrified Aaron.

Mr. Bramwell did indeed drop Gloria off the following Friday. When he parked his car and walked her the short distance to the Criterion, Aaron was already there.

"Hello, Aaron. How lovely to meet you. Andrew and Jack have told me all about you."

Aaron cringed; "Nothing too bad, I hope?"

"All good! I'm so glad you and Gloria have met."

They shook hands and, after a few more polite exchanges, David Bramwell said: "I'm off now. You two have a wonderful evening."

"I'll bring her home safe and sound, Mr. Bramwell."

"Enjoy yourselves!"

The evening was a huge success, and the first of many…

Before long, on one occasion Aaron and Gloria found themselves in his house. Gloria selected some smoochy music, put the soft lighting on and cuddled up to Aaron on the sofa. One thing led to another and they started to undress each other. Aaron was shy, nervous and panicking that he would not be able to make love to Gloria, but she took control. Her calm, loving handling of the situation, plus the confidence that the new "pill" had brought, ensured that they made love perfectly and romantically.

This boosted Aaron's confidence enormously; he felt like a man! He was no longer the thirteen-year-old boy who had been abducted by monsters! He was no longer the naïve man, who was fearful of everything, especially sex with a gorgeous woman! He was no longer a slave to tyrants! He was free, wealthy, a respected man in society, somewhat of a celebrity, and in love with the most beautiful girl he had ever seen.

After they had made love, Gloria persuaded Aaron to visit her home and meet her parents. He had briefly met her father, of course, but she wanted him to spend time with them, to get to know them, and for them to get to know him properly.

"I'm nervous with people," he fidgeted.

"You'll be fine. I'll be there!"

So, Aaron agreed.

Andrew had told the Bramwells about Aaron's shyness toward the opposite sex, because of his past – his shyness toward anyone, in fact! They were fully understanding, and hoped that the match would be a success. If it was, they would do everything they could to welcome him into their family.

"Will the fact that he's Jewish be a problem?" said Andrew.

"Well, no, we're not prejudiced in any way. I suppose it all depends on how he wants to practice his religion. I'm not sure that Gloria will want to take up Judaism!" said Mr. Bramwell.

"Well, it's early days yet, so let's see how things work out. I do know that, because of the Holocaust, Aaron has often mentioned that he no longer believes in God."

"I'm not surprised," said David.

"In which case, if things mature, they could have a civil marriage and consider religious preferences later."

"Well, we are Anglicans like you, as you know. So, Gloria can still go to church if Aaron wants to pursue his faith. Lots of couples we know worship separately."

"Well, as I said, it's early days yet; they've only just met."

Mrs. Bramwell suggested a dinner party for just the four of them. With a time and date fixed, Stephanie Bramwell planned a menu, taking heed of what was kosher, for a man she hoped would be her future son-in-law. She hadn't met him as yet, but from what she had heard she was already smitten.

Chapter 30

1968

SAN JAVIER, SPAIN

"PAPÁ, WE NEED to go! Otherwise, they will land at Alicante and we won't be there in time to meet them," said José, in a panic.

"Okay son, I'm ready."

They each drove their own cars, so there would be room to fit everyone in. The party was going to include Andrew, Jack, Joe, Clare, Aaron and Gloria.

They got there just in time, as the flight was early. They met the family and exchanged greetings, before making the journey to the villa at Santiago de la Ribera. Joe and Clare travelled with Antonio, and Aaron and Gloria travelled with José. The journey took about an hour, and both parties enjoyed the scenery, as they were given commentaries on the different places and the history of the area.

Once they had arrived, they unpacked at the villa, then ventured out for a Menu del Día in one of the local restaurants. The weather was glorious, and the visitors quickly realized that they were overdressed for the warm sunshine.

Over lunch, they discussed the engagement party. José mentioned that Mateo was a little unhappy with the party being held at the villa, in Santiago de la Ribera, and not in Alma's home. He had therefore announced that it would be held in San Cayetano, and there would be a smaller gathering for immediate family at Santiago, two days later.

"That's how he is, I'm afraid," said José: "a real Spanish patriarch. You don't argue with Mateo!"

"Well, I can understand how he feels," said Jack; "Alma is the bride to be, after all, and it is her home."

"Yes, that's not a problem," said Antonio. "It just depends what he means by 'immediate family'; he could end up bringing half of San Cayetano!"

They all laughed.

"Well, we'll cope, whatever happens. The weather is fabulous and we'll be outdoors, so it won't be a problem," said Andrew.

"I'm looking forward to it," said Aaron. "I've never been to Spain and this is all so exciting!"

"Yes, it's wonderful. I went to Mallorca two years ago, with my mum and dad, but never to mainland Spain. This is *real* Spain," said Gloria; "no tourists. Wonderful!"

They set about making a list of food. It was agreed that it would include traditional Spanish tapas. The wife of one of Antonio's employees had a catering business, and she had already agreed to prepare the food; all they had to do was make a list of the various tapas required and she would see to everything. They would get good quality wine from the local bodega, and it seemed that everything was in hand.

José drove up to San Cayetano, to see Alma and make sure everything was okay for the party. Mateo was excited and couldn't wait to meet these British millionaires! He knew all about Aaron, and had enormous sympathy for him.

"That maniac Hitler was in cahoots with that bastard Franco! They were friends. Look what they did to Guernica!"

"Shush, Mateo! How many times do I have to tell you? Sound carries, and we don't know who can hear us outside!" said Sonia.

"Bastards!"

"Just remember that this is not a democracy!"

"Yes, but this region was a republic!"

"Well, just be careful, please. I don't want the Guardia Civil knocking on our door," said Sonia.

With that, they jumped and went pale, as the front door knocked!

"Madre Mia!" Sonia scurried to the front door, and was relieved to see José.

"Come in, come in! I was just berating your father-in-law-to-be, for expressing his views about Hitler and Franco, then the door knocked! We thought it was the Guardia Civil!"

"No sign of them," José reassured; "the village is asleep."

"José, my boy, how are you?" said Mateo.

"I'm fine, thank you, señor. I just wanted to come and tell you that our guests have arrived and they're really looking forward to meeting you all. Is there anything I can do to help?"

"No, thank you; everything is in hand. Alma's in the church, talking to the sacristan; she'll be here soon. Sit down and I'll make coffee," said Sonia.

As soon as Sonia served coffee, they sat around the table in the vast kitchen area. Then the door opened and in walked Alma.

José immediately got up to embrace and kiss her. She poured herself coffee and joined them at the table. They discussed the party and any last-minute arrangements for the event, which was now two days away.

"Do you mind if I take Alma down to Santiago now, to meet Aaron and Gloria? She knows the others, but not them," said José.

"Of course not, my boy," said Mateo.

"Thank you, señor."

"I think it's time you started calling us Papá and Mamá, don't you? You're almost family now."

"Yes, of course, if that's alright."

Alma beamed, then went to get her bag. Then they said their farewells, before popping down to Santiago de la Ribera to greet her new family.

At the villa, they enjoyed more coffee and cakes, which Antonio had purchased from a local shop. Alma got to know Aaron and Gloria, and she felt confident that all of them would blend in perfectly with her family, and get along well. She couldn't wait for the day to arrive.

And, arrive it did!

Everyone gathered at the house in San Cayetano: Alma's aunts and uncles, her cousins, neighbours and friends were there, together with some of Antonio's employees, whom he respected greatly. Diego was also there with Alma's sister Isabella, who would be a bridesmaid. The village mayor and the priest, Father Pedro came along, too. Together with their British guests, there was quite a houseful for Sonia to cater for. She had worked hard and, with the help of her sisters, produced a wonderful feast.

José asked everyone for silence, then spoke:

"Hola, mis amigos… Hello, my friends. Thank you for coming tonight. As you know, I have asked Alma to marry me and she has said yes."

Everyone clapped and cheered.

"I want to thank her father and mother for allowing me to take her as my bride." He took her hand, and Alma proudly showed the ring to the gathered friends and family.

"Thanks to Señora Martinez – Mamá – and her sisters, for this wonderful food. Please raise your glasses to Alma, my wonderful fiancé."

"Salud!"

"Cheers!"

They all clapped again, then the mayor and Father Pedro both gave a little talk, after which they all enjoyed the splendid food and the wine flowed.

Andrew couldn't help noticing how quickly Father Pedro downed his first, rather large glass of wine, and how he filled his next glass almost to the brim! Good job he lived in the village! Aaron and Gloria noticed, too.

"Let's hope he'll be sober for the wedding," said Gloria.

They all laughed.

Chapter 31

1969

LONDON

"WILL YOU MARRY me, Gloria?"

"Oh, my darling, yes, I will, my love; my life!"

"I'm glad you said yes, because this ring cost a fortune!" He laughed, as she clonked him on the head with the newspaper!

He opened a box and showed her the most wonderful engagement ring. It featured a large diamond centrepiece stone, surrounded by smaller encrusted diamonds; it was dazzling. Aaron, no doubt, had an eye for such splendid jewellery, from his father's business.

"Where shall we get married?" said Gloria.

"Well, I'm happy to convert to your faith. My religion has only brought pain and sorrow – not only to me, but to the whole Jewish race," said Aaron.

Gloria looked at him for a moment, then said: "Well, there's two things to consider here: first of all, it doesn't matter what religion you convert to, you will always be Jewish! Secondly, if you no longer believe in God – as you often say, and I can fully understand why – then don't you think it's a bit deceitful to go through with Holy Baptism and Confirmation?" said Gloria.

"I still do believe in God, Gloria. I'm just cross with him sometimes, for the way we have always been persecuted!"

Gloria looked at him a second time, then said: "Well, just remember that our Jesus was Jewish, and our Christian faith was born out of Judaism. Christians, too, are persecuted in other lands; we have that in common. Perhaps it's because, between them, both faiths hold the truth. You are waiting for the Messiah to come for the first time, whereas we believe he has already come. There is a link here, between both of our faiths, so it's entirely up to you; I don't want to influence you. Whatever you do is fine with me. I will love you always."

"Thank you, darling. Let me dwell on it."

*

Aaron spoke to Andrew and Jack about it, and they were very supportive.

"It's the same god anyway, Aaron," said Andrew. "You are part of our family now, and although we have Jewish blood from our grandmother, your great aunt, we were brought up as Anglicans. Considering that your life has been stolen from you, I don't think there's any reason why you can't consider yourself an Anglican."

Aaron also spoke to Benjamin.

"No worries, mate. After what we've been through, I don't believe in any of that stuff anymore. If it means you can have a hassle-free wedding to Gloria, go for it!"

"It's much more than that, Benjy: I still believe in God, and I feel that it's better to be like the rest of my newfound family."

"Go for it then, mate!"

Benjamin had completely revoked his faith, and did everything possible to live a very un-Jewish life. He had by now come out to Aaron and the rest of the family as gay, and was now living with his boyfriend David. David was also Jewish, and had too suffered at the hands of the Nazis, but had similar feelings about his faith as Benjamin. They were happy together, and the family accepted them wholeheartedly.

So, Aaron was baptised and confirmed at the Easter Vigil on Holy Saturday, the 25th of March 1967, at Gloria's church, St. Barnabas. Her priest, Father Matthew, was absolutely thrilled, and took great delight in chatting with Aaron. As well as the confirmation classes that Aaron attended with the other candidates, Father Matthew wanted to try and make Aaron understand that he was only taking a natural step, from one set of beliefs to another. He and Aaron had many chats together, and he very skilfully instructed Aaron in the Christian faith, without making it look as if everything in the past was wrong. In the end, Aaron could see why many people believed that Jesus fulfilled the Hebrew scriptures; everything in his mind seemed to fall into place. Therefore, his conversion was not something of a convenience, just to get married in church and make things easy, but it was an actual coming to Christ.

The Bramwells were thrilled, and arrangements were made for the wedding, later that year.

The months passed quickly, and Stephanie Bramwell stepped into the role of wedding planner with great enthusiasm. The rest of the family just let her get on with it, while raising their eyebrows! Aaron didn't know much about weddings anyway, whether they were Jewish or Christian, his life having been put on hold at the age of thirteen. Gloria just shrugged her shoulders and her father laughed it all off.

Stephanie tried to continually pep talk them: "Come on, you lot! This is a big day for us, and I want it to be one to remember. You need to start taking things a bit more seriously!"

"We are, Mum, but we've got jobs to go to every day. We're happy to let you take control."

"Well, the rehearsal is next Friday, and I'm organizing a rehearsal dinner, afterwards. The best man, bridesmaids, ushers, ourselves and, of course, Father Matthew will all be here."

"That's an American thing, is it? A rehearsal meal?" said Gloria. She wondered then if it had been a good move to let her mother take full control of all the arrangements! Wedding planner, indeed!

But the day couldn't come quickly enough for Stephanie Bramwell. Anyone would think she was the one getting married, not her daughter!

The rehearsal went off very well, and there were moments of laughter, as well as moments of serious instruction, to make the day pan out perfectly. Then, they all made their way to the Bramwells' home for a sumptuous meal, overflowing with wine.

Once they were sated, an early night was suggested, so they all made their way home.

The next day was warm and sunny, and Aaron felt extremely elated about everything: his new faith, his bride and their future together.

The service in St. Barnabas was conducted by Father Matthew with great dignity. As well as the guests, there were quite a few members of the normal Sunday congregation present, as the Bramwells were faithful attenders. The flowers were stunning, the chosen music delightful and, when the bride arrived, she looked absolutely amazing.

Aaron had asked Andrew to be the best man, and they stood facing Gloria, as her dad escorted her up the aisle. Aaron wondered what his parents would think about him having converted to Christianity, but he felt sure that, given all that had happened, they would be so proud today. His gorgeous sister should be here now, he thought, as one of the bridesmaids.

The reception was held at the Rembrandt Hotel in Knightsbridge, and there were a hundred guests. Everything went according to Stephanie's plan. She beamed throughout the whole day.

Aaron and Gloria stayed at the Rembrandt Hotel that first night of their honeymoon, and the next morning they made their way to Heathrow airport, for their flight to Alicante. From there, they travelled to Santiago de la Ribera, and stayed for two weeks in the Blakes' villa. It was idyllic; the blue skies, sunshine and relaxed way of life was a wonderful experience for both of them. With money being no problem, they could have gone anywhere in the world for their honeymoon, but they chose the Mar Menor, because they wanted to just hide away and relax.

Chapter 32

1971

SAN CAYETANO, SPAIN

THE VILLAGE OF San Cayetano turned out in strength for José and Alma's wedding. In such a small village it was the wedding of the year. In fact, it had turned into part of the annual fiesta, providing an excuse for the whole village to add another event to the two-week celebration of their patron saint, which fell on 7th August. It was a full-on party, which Mateo and Sonia were only too pleased to provide.

Father Pedro conducted the ceremony with great dignity in the beautiful little church, which was attended by nearly everyone in the tiny village. It was a nuptial Mass, and the church was decorated with floral displays of white lilies, just about everywhere they could be put: they were in the porch, the baptistry, the sanctuary, and in front of every statue of Jesus and Our Lady. It looked like a flower festival!

Andrew was so moved to be asked by José to be the best man. He had grown to love his brother very much, and Alma was just delightful.

Once the ceremony was over, they all poured out of church to the reception outside.

The bunting in the church square shadowed the tables and chairs, where the reception meal was to be held. Mateo had supervised the setting up of the bar, which was provided by the nearby Bar Renato, whose back entrance was opposite the church. This was very convenient for restocking the bar, and for Renato and his family, who staffed it.

Sonia had arranged for the food to be prepared in the civic centre, by exclusive caterers, and it was transported to the church square. First of all, there was an abundance of cava served with pinchos: little, bite-sized pieces of battered pork or chicken, or tiny pastries filled with fish paté. The arrangement allowed everyone to circulate and introduce themselves to the British visitors, while eating the pinchos, washed down with plenty of cava.

The Spaniards were intrigued by the British half of the family. They had been talked about for months! Millionaires!

After some time, Mateo asked everyone to be silent, as he paid tribute to José, welcoming him into the family, and telling everyone how delighted he was to have him as a son-in-law, and how proud he was of his daughter Alma, the stunning bride. He then asked them all to be seated, and asked Father Pedro to say Grace, so that the proceedings could begin. As he offered the Grace, Jack couldn't help thinking that the priest sounded a bit tipsy, after the ever-flowing cava!

Then, the meal was served.

First, there was a mixed salad as an aperitif: huge platefuls of salad with lettuce, tomatoes, cucumber, olives, eggs, grated carrot, capers and tuna were served. There was also bread with aioli and tomato dips to accompany this.

"Good Lord, that's a meal in itself!" said Jack.

"Oh, goodness me. That's astounding," said Aaron.

Next came serrano ham, Manchego cheese, plump olives, deep-fried calamari, garlic prawns and chorizo in red wine, to choose from as entrantes. Guests could take a little of each, in true tapas style, or concentrate on one or two, however they pleased.

"Gosh, that's my diet gone!" said Gloria.

"This is just the starter!" said Clare.

"What?" said Joe. "I thought the salad was the starter!"

This was followed by gazpacho, a richly flavoured soup made from blended tomatoes, peppers, cucumber, onion, olive oil and garlic. It was served cold, with warm, crusty bread.

"How many courses do you think there are?" said Benjamin.

"Well, this is only the soup course – in my little world that's a starter!" said David.

"Well, it will all help to soak up the alcohol!" said Jack. "Look at the priest!" Father Pedro was already red in the face.

This was followed by deep-fried sardines, which were crispy and delicious.

"Oh, heavens! I'm full already," said Clare.

The next course was solomillo: a tenderloin steak, perfectly prepared to everyone's choice, and served with chips and roasted peppers.

"We won't want to eat for quite a while," said Andrew.

Throughout the meal, copious amounts of rioja were served.

Finally, there was the dessert: a tart. As each guest was served the tart, a waiter came around and poured an abundance of whisky over it!

"Oh, my god! That's got to be a full measure of whisky on each person's tart!" said Aaron.

Then there were the speeches, before coffee and liqueurs were served.

"Look at the priest!" laughed Jack.

"Oh, my goodness! If he drinks any more, he's going to collapse!" said Andrew.

The whole event was a spectacular affair. Once the meal was over, a band came. Music and dancing prevailed until the early hours of the morning, with the bar still offering free drinks.

"The priest has had it," observed Andrew.

"He's passed out," laughed Aaron. He couldn't get over it. "If this is how the Spanish celebrate special occasions, bring it on!"

"Can we move here to live?" said Gloria.

Finally, it was time to retire, and the villagers gradually made their way home. Father Pedro kind of felt his way along the church wall to the presbytery which, fortunately, was attached to the church. When only the family was left, they made their way to the various houses they were staying at.

José and Alma were taken by taxi to La Encarnacion Hotel, in Los Alcazares. From there, the next morning they would honeymoon in Italy.

"What a day to remember," said Jack.

Chapter 33

1980

LONDON

ANDREW HAD RENTED out his boutique, which now sold various other trends, and joined his dad in the charity. This pleased Jack enormously, now sixty years old.

"I wish you'd find a good woman and settle down, Andrew," said Jack, one day.

"Oh, I don't know. I just can't seem to find the right one. Anyway, I'm happy, Dad; there's so much going on."

"Why don't you try one of these new dating agencies?"

"Oh my God, no; absolutely not! I might end up with a nymphomaniac like my mother!"

They both laughed.

"Well, don't write yourself off, please."

"Don't even think of matchmaking! Remember what happened to Aunt Hilda in Neath, Clare's sister?"

One day, in his lunch break, Andrew was rapidly eating a burger and chips, which he had picked up on the high street, when the phone rang.

"Hello, Blake's Charity Foundation, Andrew Blake speaking. How can I help?"

"Hello, my name is Hank. I knew your mother during the war, when I was stationed in Cardiff. I would like to meet with you. Is that alright?"

Andrew thought this through for a moment…

"Hello, are you still there?"

"Yes, sorry. Perhaps you don't know that my mother died in 1968. She married my father in Cardiff during the war, and they moved to London."

"I know all that; you're quite a famous family! So, can we meet, please?"

"Well, yes, I suppose so. Do you want to come to the office, here at the charity?"

"Okay, that's great. When can I come?"

"Well, how about tomorrow morning, for coffee, at eleven?"

"That's great. See you then."

"Okay, goodbye... Hank, was it?"

"Yes, that's right: Hank Johnson."

Andrew rang his dad immediately, and told him all about it.

"Yes, I remember her talking about him," Jack mused. "They had a bit of a fling during the war, before I came on the scene. He was posted to Dover with his squadron and they never kept in touch. I wonder what he wants."

"Maybe he just wants to make contact after all these years, and find out what happened to Mum?"

"Hmm, I wonder..." said Jack.

"I think it would be good if you came for coffee tomorrow as well, Dad. Can you manage that?"

"Yes, I'll be there."

Andrew was restless for the rest of the day. It did all seem a bit odd. If his mother was still alive, then it might make sense for Hank to catch up, but he had never met Andrew or his dad. Alarm bells were starting to ring, and he was now glad he had asked his dad to be there.

Andrew left for work in the morning, and explained to Josie what was happening. She promised to make the coffee when Hank arrived. The coffee break couldn't come around soon enough; Andrew was intrigued. He wanted to meet this Hank and find out what this was all about.

Jack arrived at 10.30 a.m., and they caught up with a little business before Hank arrived.

On the dot of eleven, Josie buzzed through and announced Hank's arrival.

"Please send him in, Josie."

"He's on his way. I'll make the coffee."

The office door opened and in walked Hank.

He was about the same age as Jack, quite good looking and typically American.

"Howdy, I'm Hank."

"I'm Andrew and this is my dad, Jack."

"Well, that's why I'm here," said Hank, getting straight down to it: "you see, Jack isn't your father; *I* am!"

Long silence… They all stared at each other.

"Wait a minute, here," said Jack, finally. "How can you possibly say that? Myra lost touch with you when you were posted to Dover. As far as I know, you never met up again."

"Yes, we never met up again, but she did get in touch with me at the barracks and told me that she was pregnant. She said she wasn't going to say anything, and make it look as if you, Jack, were the father!"

"I don't believe you!" said Andrew. "You can't prove it. Are you after money, or what?"

"Well, my solicitor says that I should be able to claim some of Myra's fortune – as you are my son."

"Get out!" said Andrew, furiously. "Get out! You're not having a penny, and you can't prove a thing! Get out!"

"Calm down, Andrew," Jack said, quietly. "We have to do this properly, with blood tests. I'm quite happy to do that. Are you, Hank?"

"Sure thing," Hank agreed, although he didn't look all that happy about the idea.

Despite his calmness, Jack was very perturbed by the visit. When he got home, he rang one of his old friends, a retired police superintendent.

"Hello, Dave. It's Jack here."

"Hi, Jack. How nice to hear your voice! I was thinking the other day that it's time we had once of our lunches to catch up."

"Well, that's why I'm ringing: I'd like it to be sooner rather than later, as I've got a bit of a problem."

Jack explained everything, and they arranged to meet the following day, for lunch at the Criterion. Dave promised to make some investigations regarding Hank Johnson – assuming that was his real name.

"You never know," said Dave, "as an American citizen he will have entered the country as a tourist – a little bit different from the way things are now that we've joined the European Common Market. He will have to have gone through customs, and there will be a record of his entry into this country. That might help my colleagues to do a bit of searching."

Andrew was also very distressed.

"Oh, Dad, after all we've been through, I can't cope with this: having to deal with another father!"

"Oh, Andrew, try not to worry; there's no way this can be true. He's just trying to get money out of us, I'm sure of it. Knowing your mother, she probably took him to her bed, and that's why we'll need blood tests. I'll get onto it right away."

Jack arranged for the blood tests, then tried to get hold of Hank.

Hank had left his hotel address and telephone number, so he rang through. The American was out sightseeing, but he left a message with the concierge for him to ring back.

Bzzzzzz…

"Hi, Josie. What is it?"

"It's Hank on the line for you, Jack."

"Put him on."

"Jack, you asked me to call?" said Hank.

"Yes, I've arranged for us to have blood tests at St. Mary's Hospital in Paddington, tomorrow at ten a.m."

"How do I get there?"

"Get in a taxi and ask them to take you there!"

With that, Jack put the phone down.

In his hotel room, Hank stared at the telephone receiver, and thought out loud: "Hmm, the famous British politeness. We'll see, Jack Blake. We'll see."

Jack immediately phoned Joe and Clare to give them an update.

"Oh, no, not more intrigue!" Joe groaned, in dismay. "Hasn't Myra's waywardness caused enough problems?"

"I know, I know… We're getting blood tests tomorrow."

"Well, fingers crossed!"

"Yes. I'm terrified! And Andrew is absolutely distraught!"

"I'll ring him in a minute and calm him down."

"Thanks, Joe. You're the best brother-in-law anyone could have."

When Joe told Clare, she couldn't believe it.

"I told you she'd had more men than I've had hot dinners! The word 'nymphomaniac' springs to mind!"

Chapter 34

1989

LONDON

"I CAN'T BELIEVE it! It's happened, after all these years! They've been talking about it for some time now, but I didn't think it would ever really happen!" said Aaron.

"What's up? What are you talking about?" said Benjamin.

"The wall! It's come down. The Berlin Wall is no more!"

"Goodness me! Are you sure? Put the news on," said Benjamin.

They ate their lunch in the office and waited patiently for the news to come on the television. Then, at one p.m., they sat and watched the wall being demolished.

Aaron had tears in his eyes, as he witnessed the euphoria and joy of families crossing over the "border" and being reunited, after so many years.

He immediately thought of Herr Grüber. He had often felt that he wanted to return to Berlin, but the difficulties of permits and visas, plus the memories of his recapture after release from Auschwitz, put such fear into him that he had pushed all such ideas to the back of his mind. If Herr Grüber was still alive, he would be in his eighties now. And the house…? Well, who actually lived in his family's property now? His family's home.

He realized he wanted to go. He very much wanted to visit his homeland and see how things were. He wanted justice and his rightful home back. He didn't need the money, but for Aaron it was a matter of principle.

"Fancy a trip to Berlin, Benjy?"

"Wow, I don't know! Would we be allowed back?"

"Of course, silly; we're British citizens now. Gloria would love it and my son will just be made up, I think."

"Well, I'd love to go, I must say. Can David come, too?"

"I'll speak to Gloria; we can all go together if you like. I'm sure

David will be up for it, won't he?"

"I'm sure he will be; I'll work on him. He might be a bit wary, as all his family were murdered on Kristallnacht. He was lucky to escape, and later found his way here on a Kindertransport."

So, in a few days' time, all was arranged; Gloria and Aaron travelled with Benjamin and his boyfriend David to Berlin.

Aaron and Gloria's son Rueben (named after Aaron's father) agreed to stay behind and run the family business, which had grown successfully over the years. The Goldberg fortune was being put to good use, helping refugees from all corners of the world, seeking asylum from tyrannical regimes. Also, the Blake Charity Foundation continued to help the homeless. It now owned a number of small properties in various parts of London, and was in a position to house clients temporarily, until they were established in employment. The two charities sometimes crossed paths, as refugees were often not able to set themselves up immediately, and to avoid begging and living on the streets, Aaron would often refer some of his clients to Andrew.

The quartet of travellers stayed in the Hampton Hilton, Berlin Alexanderplatz Hotel.

Aaron and Benjamin were astounded at the growth of the city, and the renovations to important landmarks. It gave David the creeps when he recognized the streets, which were covered in broken glass the last time he was in this city. He thought of his whole family killed in the upstairs apartment of their shop. His father was a tailor, and the family had run a successful business. On the night of Kristallnacht, his mother had made him flee before the brownshirts had come, smashing windows and vandalizing everything inside all the Jewish properties. David went with other children in the neighbourhood and hid in safety, in the nearby park, from where they could see their local synagogue burning. He immediately thought of the psalm he had been taught the Sabbath before it, in kinder school: "Psalm 74"; the verses had stuck in his mind...

"The enemy has laid waste the whole of the sanctuary.
Your foes have made uproar in your house of prayer:
they have set up their emblems, their foreign emblems,
high above the entrance to the sanctuary.
Their axes have battered the wood of its doors.
They have struck together with hatchet and pickax.
O God, they have set your sanctuary on fire;
they have razed and profaned the place where you dwell.
They said in their hearts: 'Let us utterly crush them;
let us burn every shrine of God in the land.'"

The children waited for two days, hiding in bushes in the extensive park, until they felt it was safe to return home. Alas, when they dared to go back, all they could see was broken glass on the streets and properties devastated. The neighbours told him that, although some families had survived, unfortunately his father had been thrown out of the bedroom window of their top floor apartment, to his death. His mother had rushed down the stairwell to help him, but had been shot when she reached him.

One of the neighbours told him to find a certain Englishman, who was living in a hotel in Berlin, and was trying to arrange transport to England for Jewish children. He gave him the name of the hotel, David removed his Star of David and, along with the other children he had been hiding with, made his way through central Berlin to the hotel. Fortunately, the man was still at the hotel and David, along with the other children, was successful in eventually arriving in Great Britain.

The whole situation was a nightmare and he had never fully grieved for his parents and grandparents. Even now, in adulthood, it gave him nightmares to think of their terrible deaths. It was only the fear of being caught and the friendship of other children on the transport which kept him from despair. Reaching England and making a new life erased all memories and helped greatly, so returning to Berlin now was a huge challenge for him. But he wanted to be here. He wanted to face his haunted past.

After a superb dinner at the hotel, they went out for a bit of sightseeing. Gloria loved it all, having never been to Berlin before.

Aaron, Benjamin and David, though, had other fascinations!

The next day, they made their way to what was until recently the eastern sector, and soon found themselves outside number 13, Hans-Otto-Straffe.

Herr Grüber's name was still on the array of names on the new modern intercom system, and Aaron pressed the button in trepidation.

An elderly man answered and Aaron gave his name. The door buzzed open and they entered the hallway, to find Herr Grüber coming down the stairs to greet them.

"Aaron, my boy! How wonderful to see you again! I've been reading all about you in the newspapers, now that we are free and that wretched wall has come down."

"You look well, Herr Grüber," said Aaron.

"Well, I'm eighty-three now, but battling on, you know."

Aaron introduced his wife Gloria and his friends, Benjamin and David. Herr Grüber ushered them in and took them up to his apartment.

He opened a bottle of Riesling. "It's not a very good one, I'm afraid. Luxuries are hard to come by in this stark environment. Hopefully, things will change now that we are free."

"It's fine," said Aaron. "It's very good of you to even think of it."

"Not at all, my boy. You deserve better!"

They had a good chat. Herr Grüber told them that he was the only resident left of the original tenants. The "old bat", who had been so rude to Aaron the last time he came, had moved elsewhere, and there were four new families and one apartment vacant.

"Well, Herr Grüber—"

"Please, call me Otto."

"Well, Otto, who actually owns the place now?"

"It's still owned by the government. Now that we're free of that wall, you should put a claim in. Have you still got those documents?"

"No, the Soviet officer who arrested me took them, and I've never seen them since."

"Well, we'll see about that. I have copies of most of them. Your father was a very astute man, Aaron; he had copies made and gave them to me. I had to hide them under the floorboards in my old apartment, for fear those ignorant Nazi thugs would ever find them, but I still have them."

"That's astonishing, Otto! I can't believe that!"

"Well, I'll go and get them for you, before you go. Now, tell me all about yourself."

Aaron, Gloria, Benjamin and David chatted with Otto for quite a while, and another bottle of Riesling was opened, as Otto told them all about stark living under communist rule.

"All things in common, my foot!" said Otto. "All things for those who grabbed and kept for themselves, while the ordinary folk went without, and you dare not say anything or you'd end up in Siberia! In many ways they were almost as bad as those filthy Nazis!"

"Well, there's a new dawn breaking now," said Benjamin.

"Yes," said David. "thank goodness."

They all chatted happily. Gloria, Benjamin and David were very taken with Otto.

When it was time to leave, Otto retrieved the documents. There were a few photos, but most importantly Rueben had paid to have official copies of his and Esther's wedding certificate, together with all of their birth certificates. There was also a copy of the deeds of the house, which clearly named Rueben and Esther as the rightful owners. Aaron and Gloria were stunned, and took them with gratitude.

"I always had a feeling that one day they would be needed. I'm just so sorry that all your lovely family had to perish for a stupid ideology, and in such a horrific, monstrous way. The 'Master Race'!" fumed Otto.

They bade Otto farewell and promised to keep in touch.

"Lovely to see you again, Otto. We'll keep in touch, I promise," said Aaron.

"God bless you, Aaron. Lovely to meet you all."

"What a lovely man," said Gloria, after they had left. "How kind of him to keep all those copies."

"He was a wonderful neighbour, and very fond of my family. His wife and my grandmother were inseparable."

They returned to the hotel.

Over dinner, they discussed whether Aaron should make a claim on the house.

"We don't need the money, that's for sure; but it is a matter of principle," said Aaron.

"Yes, you're absolutely right; it's your family home by right. Besides, imagine if poor old Otto was told to leave, at his age. You know the trouble with tenancies," said Gloria.

"Well, at least if you were the landlord you could make sure that never happened. In fact, you could probably let the other apartments out to needy people, as they become vacant," said Benjamin.

"Yes, a kind of expansion of the charity in London," said David.

"Well, let's see what Rueben, Andrew and Jack think about it, when we get back. We've got enough contacts at home to set any claim in process," said Aaron.

On their last day, David wanted to visit the street where he lived with his family.

They made their way to Kurfürstendamm, which was famous for its exclusive shops and nightlife. He couldn't believe the transformation, from the destruction he had witnessed as a boy.

They all stood before a memorial to the horror, and said a prayer. It helped David a lot, though he held back the tears. Then, they went shopping for gifts to take home for the family. Gloria wanted to buy something nice for their son, Reuben, and Aaron wanted to take something home for Jack and Andrew. They visited several department stores.

As they came out of the Kaufhaus des Westens department store, Benjamin stopped dead in his tracks and froze.

"What's the matter, Benjy?" said David. "You look as if you've seen a ghost!"

"Look over there… on that bench…"

"What is it?"

"Not a ghost… A Nazi monster! I recognize him from Treblinka!"

"Are you sure?" said Aaron.

"I could never forget that face, even after all these years! He was the most sadistic bastard! I can still see him now, whipping a man to death. I'm going over there to confront him."

"No, don't do that! It could be dangerous," said Gloria.

"Yes, especially if he's just someone who looks like the man you remember!" said David.

"I've got an idea: better to walk past and be sure it's him, then pretend to be taking photos of the park behind him; when he goes back to reading his newspaper, you can take one of him surreptitiously. If he looks up, quickly resume snapping the park," suggested Aaron.

"That sounds like a great idea. Let's do it."

They went back into the department store and bought a Polaroid camera. Then, they all crossed the road together and walked past the man, after which Benjamin was more convinced than ever. They kept together in a crowd, as tourists do, and spoke in English, so the man would be convinced of their tourist status.

Benjamin did exactly what Aaron had suggested. Then, when the man seemed happy that tourists were photographing the park, Benjamin quickly took one of him. The man didn't even notice, he had become so used to the click of the camera.

They decided to take the photograph to the Jewish Restoration Office. Benjamin knew the name he went by and his nickname: his real name was Hans Beiker, but he was better known as "Beiker the Beast".

The authorities in the Restoration Office took a long time to interview Benjamin. They wanted to know his history and the details of his family. They were able to trace his identity, and records of the death of his family in Treblinka, and this all gave credence to his belief that Beiker was at large. They kept the photograph, and details of Benjamin's address and telephone in London. They promised to keep him informed of any conviction, and advised him that he may have to return to Berlin, to testify in a possible trial. Benjamin said that he was only too happy to do that, remembering the people he saw dying in agony from Beiker's frenzied whipping.

After a few more hours of sightseeing, which included a visit to the Holocaust Memorial and the Jewish Museum, they returned to the hotel for dinner. Then, the next day, they flew back to London, eager to tell their news to the rest of the family.

Chapter 35

1990

SAN JAVIER, SPAIN

"I DON'T KNOW, Papá; I'm not sure. I was very angry when I left them, to make a new life with you."

"I know, José, but I've heard from the solicitor who helped me search for you, and he says that the woman you called Mama for twenty-four years is terminally ill with cancer. I think you should try and find it in your heart to forgive them."

"Well, let me think about it for a bit. They probably won't want to see me, anyway; I said some awful things as I was leaving."

"I know, and while that's understandable, it's also why I think you should make the effort to go and see them. I'll come with you, don't worry. You see, I'm only drawing your attention to this because the solicitor made further investigations after you left with me, on that dreadful day. They didn't really know the circumstances; they were told by the priest that you were an orphan, and that your parents had died when you were a baby."

"But the priest sold me to them!"

"Well, yes, money was exchanged, but the solicitor says that they thought they were giving a donation to the church, in return for giving an orphan a home."

Silence…

"Oh, God! Why didn't they say all that at the time?"

"They were too shocked, upset and baffled by me turning up with a solicitor and the Guardia Civil, with all the documents proving that I was your father. I feel guilty as hell, really."

"Well, don't feel guilty; you didn't know, either. Yes, okay, I'll go."

"It took years for the solicitor to find me; the Guardia Civil wouldn't help. He had a vague idea that I came from the Mar Menor area, but the nuns in the hospital in Santiago de la Ribera were not forthcoming. The one who had given me information was even reprimanded!"

José was really depressed now, and on the verge of tears. He'd had a good upbringing with Gabriella and Miguel, and hadn't wanted for anything. He felt guilty; he should have contacted them before, and not left it for so many years.

"We'll all go," said Alma.

"Yes, that would be good. After all, José, they gave you a good home and they loved you. You loved them, too, and they brought you up to be the fine young man that I met when I came to claim you as my own," said Antonio.

"Yes, I know it was a terrible time, but I quickly came to love you, because blood is thicker than water; knowing my true family history made me feel complete. It was like a yearning that had been fulfilled, because I knew I was an 'orphan', and there's always that nagging desire to find one's roots. However, look at what's happened since: I have an extended family in Great Britain, my darling Alma, with our gorgeous Lucia, and a real father."

"We're going, and we're taking Lucia with us," said Alma.

Jose had a sleepless night. He was nervous about meeting up with them, and full of heartache that he had never known they were also innocent victims of the "niños rosados" scandal. Alma reassured him that they would be overjoyed to meet up, and that reconciliation would be a very good thing for everyone – especially his adoptive mother, dying of cancer.

He had to admit that he had thought about them often, and was sorry that he had not kept in touch – after all, as Antonio said, they had given him a good home; no better than Antonio and his grandmother Maria would have given him but, under the circumstances, nevertheless a home. He could have been sold to a worthless family and been abused, or grown up on the wrong side of the tracks.

He woke up happy for Antonio and Alma to make all the arrangements with the solicitor. Although heart-aching, it would bring peace to the situation, and closure to an open wound.

Chapter 36

1990

BERLIN

"WELL, I CAN'T believe I own our family home again!" said Aaron.

"It's rightfully yours, darling; the authorities didn't have a leg to stand on, with all the evidence and documents you provided, together with Otto's testimony. To think, this was all only made possible because of the collapse of the Berlin Wall!" said Gloria.

"Mama and Papa would be so happy to know about this. I could cry for the way things were in those dark days."

"I know, darling. But they are looking down on us and can see it all unfolding."

"I know; I still have a faith – even more so since I've become an Anglican," said Aaron. "But I still get very angry when I think back: how can any God allow such evil to happen in a world he claims to have created and loves?"

"All the evil in this world is the Devil's doing: enticing people to destroy God's beautiful world; influencing them to acts of violence and hatred, in small ways and on large scale, like world wars," said Gloria.

"You really believe that, don't you?"

"Yes. You are one of the Chosen People, and the Devil wants to eliminate you all. I've read a lot of Hebrew theology since I married you, and I firmly believe this. The Christian faith is born out of Judaism – that's why we're persecuted too, in other lands."

"I'd never thought of it like that," said Aaron. "Yes, we've been persecuted since Pharaoh made us slaves, in Egypt."

"And it's going to continue, as long as the world is in the Devil's grip! We've just got to fight against it. There will always be groups of neo-Nazis rising up, and there will always be those with nationalistic sympathies – it's the Devil's doing! If we don't fight it, such nationalistic feelings will bring about another Nazi state."

"Yes, you're right."

"Come on. Hurry up and pack or we'll miss the flight," said Gloria.

"I can't wait to tell Otto the good news. I'm going to ask him to keep an eye on the property for us, and let us know if there are any problems."

"That's a good idea... But remember he's eighty-odd!"

"He's a sprightly old thing, though. And, remarkably, he's computer literate for his age; we communicate by email."

"Well, that's going to make things much easier," said Gloria.

They finished packing and waited for the taxi to take them to Heathrow.

The flight was delayed, so they had to waste an hour at the airport. Aaron took the opportunity to catch up with some business, emailing and telephoning his son Rueben. Eventually, they were ready to board the plane.

After they had settled into their seats, they both had a short snooze. Before they knew it, they were landing.

"Let's book in and get unpacked at the hotel, before we visit Otto," suggested Aaron. "Perhaps we could take him out for dinner. He's done so much for me, and has been a loyal family friend, before and after the Nazi regime."

"Yes, that's a lovely idea."

They booked into the same hotel in Alexanderplatz as when they came out with Benjamin and David. Then, they made their way to 13 Hans-Otto-Straffe. They had already emailed Otto, so he knew they were coming.

He was ready for them. After hugs and kisses, they left his apartment.

"Did they name this street after you, Otto?" laughed Aaron.

"Yes, it's funny that, isn't it? No, I'm a nobody."

"You're anything but a 'nobody'; you've been a loyal friend to our family."

"Well, I'm lucky the Nazis didn't pick me up, too; I wasn't very accommodating when it came to interrogations."

"Gosh, I didn't think you had to go through anything like that. I'm sorry, Otto. What was it all about?"

"They banged on the door in the middle of the night, as was their way. It was the Gestapo, of course, and we thought the worst. They thoroughly searched the old house across the road, where we lived, and I was terrified they would find the copies of your documents. They thought I was hiding jewellery, which your dad had given me."

"Really?" said Gloria.

"What happened?" asked Aaron.

"Well, they turned the house upside down. Of course, they didn't find anything because, although your dad said he was going to give me jewellery to hide, in case you ever made it back, he was never able to do so; they had already stolen everything from his shop. Fortunately, I had a heavy chest of drawers over the loose floorboards, where the documents were hidden. It was touch and go though, I can tell you. It put years on my wife, Heidi! It wasn't long after that she had a stroke and died. She couldn't cope with the life we had to live."

"Oh, dear, I am so sorry!" said Gloria.

"Well, she didn't enjoy good health; I think she would never have survived the bombing, and the devastation it brought. We never blamed the Allies, of course; everyone could see that it was what that lunatic Hitler had brought upon us."

They made their way to a restaurant Aaron had been told about, in what was the western sector; although things were improving on the eastern side, it had a way to go yet. The restaurant was very modern, offering traditional German fare. Once seated, a waitress came over and they ordered their food and wine.

"Well, Otto, I've got some news for you: thanks to you saving those documents, I've been able to prove that number thirteen is my property. And it's all down to you, my dear friend."

"Oh, Aaron, my boy, that's wonderful!"

"So, I'm your new landlord. And there's no way that you will ever have to leave that apartment!"

Otto burst into tears, and Gloria grasped hold of his hand. He was overwhelmed, but so grateful for the security this news provided. There was always the threat that the communists would evict them and put such a grand building to another use.

"I'm going to give you the apartment, Otto. But I've got a huge favour to ask, in return."

"Oh, Aaron, you mustn't do that! It's your family home!"

"Nonsense! It's seen so many changes, with the Nazis and the Soviets, and it is now six apartments; it can never be thought of as a family home ever again. The apartment is yours, for all of your kindness, friendship and loyalty to my family and myself."

"Oh, goodness me; that's so kind of you! So, what is the favour you want?"

"Well, I just want you to keep an eye on the place, and make sure nobody paints their apartment black with pink spots, or knocks walls through – that sort of thing, you know. You can just email me any concerns, and I'll fly over and deal with them. The income from the other tenants will go into an account which will be yours, and you will have the authority to use the money for any renovations you feel are needed. Just keep me up to date; I'll always be happy to help."

Otto started to cry again. This time Aaron took hold of him, and they embraced.

"This is going to give me a new lease of life, Aaron! Thank you so much!"

"It's a happy ending to some tragic stories, hopefully. And, if it wasn't for you, none of it would be at all possible. Thank you, my dear friend."

Chapter 37

1990

SAN JAVIER, SPAIN

"I CAN'T WAIT to get this over and done with, Papá; I'm nervous, guilty as hell, and more than a little bit frightened!"

"You're not on your own with the guilty feeling, son; remember, I was the one who came to claim you back! Don't worry, José; only good can come from this. If it gives Gabriella peace of mind before she dies, then it's going to be a healing mission. I think, though, that we must keep in touch with them after this. In fact, we should think about going to the funeral when the times comes, if that's possible. After that, we should keep in touch with Miguel also, I feel."

"Absolutely," said Alma.

"Yes, you're right; we need to make amends," said José.

They enjoyed the journey to Barcelona. The changing countryside was astonishing, as they moved through the different regions. It was a long way, but they stopped off several times for coffee, lunch and nature calls.

Once they had arrived, José drove straight to the hotel he had booked them into. It was one that he knew was well recommended, from when he was growing up in Barcelona as a boy. After booking in, they went for a walk along the seafront, to enjoy the famous sights. Alma and Lucia were delighted, as they had never been to Barcelona before.

José's emotions were in turmoil, as memories of the happy life he'd enjoyed with Gabriella and Miguel came rushing back to him. The guilt was weighing him down and it was showing on his face.

"I know that look, "said Alma. "Stop it, right now! The only person who needs to feel guilty here is that wretched priest! In fact, the whole bloody Church – and that murdering Franco!"

"Absolutely," said Antonio. "But watch your language in front of Lucia, please!"

"Sorry, Papá!"

"Well, let's go back to the hotel for dinner now and get a good sleep, because tomorrow is going to be quite an emotional day," said José.

"I'm so glad you and Lucia are with us, Alma – I really am. It's going to show Gabriella and Miguel that José's new life has been a good thing," said Antonio.

At the hotel, they enjoyed their meal together, and very soon Antonio was happy to retire to his room to watch T.V.; it had been a long journey. The others, however, went to the spa centre at the hotel, and had a great time in the swimming pool, sauna and jacuzzi. Then, they had some drinks at the poolside bar afterward. It was a luxurious setting.

"Papá, I love it here!" said Lucia. "Can we come and have holidays here? I'm fed up with travelling to cold, cloudy London!"

José and Alma laughed.

"She's got a point, José!" she said. "If we're going to keep in touch with Gabriella and Miguel, we could make it an annual trip. This hotel is wonderful."

"Please, Papá!" said Lucia.

"Well, yes," he agreed, "I don't think that's a bad idea at all."

"Yeeesss!" said Lucia, then jumped back into the water, splashing her mother and father.

"Hey, you, calm down!" said Alma.

The next day dawned and, after a sumptuous breakfast, they made their way to the home of Miguel and Gabriella Sanchez.

José's stomach turned as they approached the house. It was a modest villa, but a comfortable home, with so many happy memories for José. The lawyer had arranged the meeting, so Miguel and Gabriella knew they were coming.

José rang the doorbell and they waited.

Gabriella opened the door and immediately burst into tears as she looked at José. He hugged her and sobbed, too.

"I'm sorry… so sorry that I've treated you this way!" said José. "I should never have cut you out of my life, after all you did for me and the happy life you gave me!"

"Don't worry, José; none of this is your fault! We were bewildered by the whole situation, but we have missed you so much. We have tried on several occasions to make contact with you, to explain things, but the Church authorities clamped down and said no information could be found."

"Yes, they wouldn't want to admit their crimes! However, one day the truth will out; we're all victims here," said Antonio.

Miguel came to the door and embraced José. More tears flowed. Finally, they went inside the villa.

They had lots to talk about. They chatted about José's real mother, Myra, and her atrocious behaviour. They spoke about his new extended family in England, his wife Alma and their daughter, Lucia. Then, they talked about life in Santiago de la Ribera and London.

Gabriella explained that they genuinely thought that his adoption was a project funded by the Church, to help orphans. They were advised to make a donation to the project, for the privilege of having a beautiful baby boy to call their own – a particular sum of money was suggested.

"There is no way that we felt we were buying you, José – no way at all. It was dressed as a donation to the Church, to help the project give homes to more orphans," said Miguel.

They talked about Gabriella's deteriorating health, and how this reunion had brought such peace of mind to her. She had been told treatment would be discontinued – an effective death sentence – and was dealing with it very courageously. Miguel, however, was not coping very well at all. There were more tears and hugs at this.

"Well, let's try and make a new start now. We must keep in touch by telephone and email, as often as we can, while we have the chance, and we must come up and meet with you again soon. Lucia here is very taken with Barcelona; she declared yesterday that she's fed up with visiting cold, cloudy London!" said José.

They all laughed.

"Oh, yes, please, that would be wonderful!" said Gabriella. "We must keep in touch."

She served a wonderful tapas lunch and they continued to catch up on various aspects of their lives, which both parties had missed out on. Gabriella was particularly taken with Alma and Lucia, and wanted to know all about her family and the village of San Cayetano.

"I wish I was well enough to travel, and to meet your family and see the place. We had a holiday in Mazarron some years ago, which we really enjoyed, but we've never been to the Mar Menor. I hear it is lovely, and developing rapidly into a tourist area."

"Well, if you speak to your doctor and ask his advice, perhaps he may allow you to make the journey," said Alma.

"We'll see," said Gabriella, but she knew it was impossible. She was sure she didn't have long to go.

After lunch they relaxed in the lounge, chatting until it was time to leave.

They promised to call again in the morning for coffee, before leaving for Santiago de la Ribera. With more hugs and kisses, Miguel led them to the front door.

Outside, José said quietly: "Keep us informed on everything. When the time comes, we intend on coming to the funeral."

"That would be wonderful, José; she would love that. Thank you all so much for coming; it has given her a boost and put her mind at peace."

They returned to the hotel and enjoyed another night in luxury.

Lucia loved it. She dragged her mother and father to the spa again, while Antonio enjoyed the comfort of his room and television.

José slept better that night.

In the morning, after another enormous breakfast, they went to the Sanchez house for coffee, as promised, before leaving for home.

Chapter 38

1992

BERLIN

"ARE YOU HANS Beiker?"

"Yes, I am. What do you want?"

"We have a warrant for your arrest, for the ill-treatment and murder of Jews in Treblinkla concentration camp, and for complicity in the genocide of the Jewish race: the 'Final Solution'."

Silence… then explosion:

"How dare you come here accusing me of this! I have only recently buried my wife; Karl, my son and I are still in mourning! Go away and leave me alone!"

"There are millions of Jews in mourning, too, after your criminal behaviour!" said the police officer.

"Who is there, Dad? What's going on?" called Karl Beiker, from the back of the house.

"It's the police, son. They've come to arrest me!"

"What?!"

Karl Beiker rushed to the front door and confronted them. "What do you think you're doing?! Who do you think you are?! My father is eighty-five years old, recently bereaved and a loyal German citizen. What on Earth do you think he's guilty of?"

"We have a warrant for his arrest, for war crimes and atrocities committed during the Nazi regime. He will have the opportunity to defend himself in court; now he needs to come with us quietly, and let justice take its course."

"What war crimes?! He was just a soldier on the front line during the war."

"I'm afraid we have evidence that he was at Treblinka concentration camp, and was complicit in acts of brutality."

"No, Dad. Tell them this is all lies!"

But Hans Beiker had turned white, and couldn't seem to get his words out. A stunned Karl Beiker pleaded with the police that this could only be a huge mistake.

In the end, he was allowed to accompany his ashen-faced father to the police station. Once they had arrived there, Hans Beiker was officially charged, before being taken to Berlin's Moabit prison. Karl Beiker was allowed to make the journey with him.

Before they got into the police car, his father told him to say nothing within earshot of the police. Karl was confused, and couldn't understand what he meant, but heeded his father's words, nonetheless.

When they arrived at the prison, Hans Beiker was processed, given prison garments and escorted to his cell.

Karl was not allowed to see him, and was told that he could visit him at the official visiting time later, in the visitors' area. So he went to a local bar, where he felt like drinking the sea dry.

After a few hours, he returned to the prison to visit his father.

"Dad, we'll sort this out. There's been a huge mistake here. This is outrageous!"

"Listen, son, I want you to go into the attic at home and destroy what's there. Don't ask me any questions now; I need to think. Just gather everything up and dispose of it all. I'll explain later, but for now it is imperative that you do as I say, as quickly as possible."

Karl's stomach churned, and he had a profound feeling of foreboding. What was this all about?

"Go now, please! Come back tomorrow; I shall explain everything. The key to the attic is in a canister, on the top shelf of the larder unit in the kitchen."

So, Karl left the prison and made his way home, his mind working overtime.

He had never been in the attic. It just seemed to him a place for storing junk. His mother always said there was nothing much up there.

He found the key and, using the step ladder from the garage, climbed up to the attic opening, in the ceiling of the landing. When he opened it, with a torch he could see that there was a ladder which could be lowered to the floor – this made things easier. Once he had lowered it, he made his way up the ladder and into the attic space.

He could see that it was rather larger than the average attic; he was able to stand upright. He saw a door facing him. There was a light switch on the wall outside it, which he turned on. Then, using the key, he opened the door and stepped inside.

For a moment, he stood speechless. He felt instant panic; his heart started to beat faster.

It was a room, but one which might better be described as a shrine to Nazism.

And there, on a mannequin in the corner, was his father's uniform, the dreaded swastika armband on one of the sleeves.

A huge Nazi flag emblazoned one wall. There were photos of his father with Hitler and other high-ranking Nazis, pinned to display boards on the other walls. There were also medals he had been awarded, and two box files on a table. The most frightening thing of all was probably a coiled bullwhip, hanging from a hook.

Karl couldn't believe his eyes. His mother and father had always told him that he was an ordinary soldier, who was lucky enough to return from the Russian front line.

There was a chair before him, so he sat down and reached for the box files. The first contained two photograph albums. He opened the first album and flicked through photos of his father attending rallies and meetings, once again with Hitler and other high-ranking Nazis. There were more disturbing photos, of his father and mother at dinners and celebratory occasions. His wonderful, homely mother mixing with Nazi officials!

He was utterly dismayed. Karl was born after the war, and had grown up accepting his mother and father's explanation of how things were: that he was a common soldier obeying his orders.

The second album was nothing less than devastating. It showed photos of Treblinka concentration camp. There were grainy images of the emaciated inmates, the gas chambers, the piles of corpses and… one of a guard whipping a naked man.

Karl looked more closely at the guard, then suddenly up at the whip on the wall. He thought he was starting to have palpitations. Aloud, he said: "Oh, God, please, no!"

The second box was full of papers: official documents from the German High Command – some were signed by Rheinhard Heydrich, some by Heinrich Himmler. All of them gave instructions regarding the extermination of the Jews.

Karl was crying by now, and wondering what on Earth to do. He loved his dad, and the memory of his beloved mother was prominent in his mind and heart, following her recent death. He couldn't betray his father… could he? Yet, he knew that the sight of everything before him would haunt him forever!

He nearly jumped out of his skin when the doorbell rang.

He wiped away his tears and composed himself. Then, he made his way down the ladder to the front door. On opening the door, he was met by police officers holding a search warrant.

He didn't need to wonder what to do anymore; the decision had been made for him. He didn't have to agonize over whether to betray his father or dispose of the evidence; the evidence was appalling and there for all to see. As the police searched the house, of course they could not fail to see the open attic, with the light on and a ladder leading up to it. When they saw the contents of the hidden room, they telephoned for help to gather the material, to take away as evidence.

"Your father has kept this shrine to the most evil period in the history of the world," one of the officers said, with contempt. "It is shameful to German history!"

"Officer, I honestly knew nothing about this; I only just this moment opened the attic, because my father asked me to dispose of everything. I didn't know what he meant, and I had no idea what I would find; when I opened the attic I was stunned. This has come as a great shock to me."

"Well, you will need to give evidence in court."

In a short time, more officers came. They packed everything up and took it all away.

After they had left, Karl burst into tears again, and sat there, sobbing.

"Oh, Dad, you foolish old man! Why keep all of that evil rubbish in our lovely home?"

He had a sleepless night; he was dreading going to the prison the next morning. He had been taught in school about the horrors of the Holocaust, and now that it was on his doorstep, he couldn't believe it.

He couldn't face breakfast. After nothing more than a couple of cups of coffee, he made his way to the prison.

"Well son, did you do as I asked?"

"Dad, I couldn't: the police came with a search warrant while I was in the attic. They've taken everything away. There is nothing I could do."

"Oh, I see. Well, then, that's the end of me…" Hans looked reflective.

"How could you have been involved in such atrocities?" Karl demanded. "Those photos, the documents… It's a nightmare!"

"If we didn't comply and obey orders, then we would have ended up in the gas chambers ourselves! It was a terrifying time."

"I have an awful feeling that the photo of a man whipping another… is you, holding the whip… the whip that was hanging on the wall in our home."

His father was silent.

"How could you? How could you have kept that whip, like some kind of souvenir?"

Silence.

"You're a sick man!"

"We were all caught up in this hatred! We were brainwashed into believing that the Jews had caused all of Germany's problems."

"But, why such brutality? It's inhuman!"

Beiker's lawyer advised him to plead guilty; it would have been foolish to try denying the charges, with such overwhelming items on display in the courtroom.

Because of the evidence, the court case only lasted a few weeks. The documents, photos and the whip were all conclusive in condemning him as the sadist who had inflicted such suffering on his innocent victims.

Then, of course, there was Benjamin's testimony, after a frustratingly long investigation. Having chased up his report on numerous occasions, he was delighted to finally hear about the arrest, and had gladly travelled to Berlin to give evidence. Furthermore, two more survivors had come forward, following all the publicity since the arrest, and they confirmed everything. It came out that he was known as "Beiker the Beast"; all testified to his brutality.

Beiker was condemned to prison for the rest of his life.

Karl was to be heard sobbing in the gallery, at the verdict.

*

After the trial, Hans's son didn't think he could live with this knowledge; it was overwhelming. He put the house on the market and moved to another area of Berlin.

He regularly visited his father in prison and, as time passed, he could see that Hans was deteriorating. It wouldn't be long, he knew, before Beiker the Beast would meet his maker.

Karl himself would suffer with acute depression, and live as a recluse for the rest of his life.

Chapter 39

1993

LONDON

AARON WAS SURPRISED that Benjamin was late for their meeting. It wasn't like him; he was always punctual.

The phone rang.

"Hello, Goldberg Charity here; Aaron Goldberg speaking. How can I help?"

"You're next, Jewboy!"

The phone went dead.

Aaron was bewildered and suddenly in a panic, as his heart beat faster. The last time he was called "Jewboy" was in Berlin as a lad, then Auschwitz. What on Earth did this mean?

He paced his office, feeling uneasy.

The phone rang again.

He looked at it, wondering whether to answer it or not.

After endless rings, he picked up the receiver.

"Yes?" he croaked.

"Aaron? It's Andrew."

He sighed in relief. "Hello, Andrew."

"Have you heard the news?" Andrew sounded shaken, and Aaron was immediately on edge.

"No, what?"

"You should sit down… Benjy's been murdered."

"What?! Where?! How?!"

"He was stabbed, on his way home from shopping. He'd been to the supermarket, to get some things for a meal he and David were planning tonight; he was attacked and stabbed, not far from his house. David is in a terrible state; we need to go to him."

"Oh, my god! This is terrible! Who can have done a thing like this? He was harmless."

"There was a note stuck to his jacket. It said: *'Revenge'*!"

"Revenge?! For what?"

There was silence... Andrew didn't want to say it to Aaron.

"Oh, God! Do you think this is linked to Beiker's conviction?"

"Yes, I do," said Andrew, simply.

Aaron told Andrew about the phone call he had received moments before he called. Andrew was immediately launched into action.

"I'm coming over right away! You need police protection – we need to sort that out."

"Well, my secretary is here, and a few other members of staff."

"A madman with a knife could easily walk in and ask to see you, pretending to be a refugee seeking help. Come on, Aaron; you're in a very vulnerable position."

"I suppose so. Oh, God. Does this anti-Semitism ever go away?" He thought of Gloria's words, when they went to Berlin to visit Otto.

"Stay put; I'm on my way," said Andrew. "Then we'll go to David, then the police."

"Okay."

Aaron put the phone down and fell into his chair. He was ashen – anxious, nervous and frightened. He had a dreadful feeling of foreboding.

Andrew made his way to Aaron's offices.

Before going in to see Aaron, he spoke to the receptionist and the other members of staff: he told them what had happened to Benjamin, and of Aaron's threatening phone call. He warned them of the danger, but assured them that they were going to the police to seek help, and ask for police protection. They were all very concerned, but promised to be careful, agreeing that there should be greater security in the office.

Andrew went into Aaron's office, and found him with his head in his hands. He had been crying. He immediately hugged Andrew.

"After all we've been through... why this, now?"

"I know, mate. But we'll sort it out. I promise."

"Nothing can bring Benjy back! And, what about David? He's probably at risk, too."

"Have you told Gloria?"

"No, I'd rather tell her face to face. I suppose we're all at risk, really."

"Come on, let's go and see David."

*

They rang the doorbell of David and Benjamin's apartment, and a policeman answered the door. They explained who they were and were ushered inside.

David collapsed in Aaron's arms, sobbing like a baby.

"Why, why, why?! I can't believe it! He's suffered so much in the past – we all have! The police are convinced it's because of Beiker's conviction and subsequent life imprisonment; members of his family must have sought Benjy out, after his testimony in court. After all, it made sensational worldwide headlines."

The police officer said to David: "I think you should stay with someone for a few days, or have someone stay here with you, sir. We have a few leads; hopefully this crime can be solved quite quickly.

"There is an extreme right-wing group called 'Britannica Yes', who have been demonstrating their hatred and committing crimes against Jews and black people. Hopefully we can round them up, find some answers and, with any luck, disband them."

"Wow! I've never heard of them. They sound like a neo-Nazi group. Do you suppose someone in Beiker's family will have made contact with them?"

"Yes, that's possible, sir. We've made some investigations with the police in Berlin. Beiker has a son, although apparently he was devastated by his father's crimes, and has become something of a recluse. There doesn't seem to be any other family… but, who knows? The police in Berlin are making thorough investigations."

"But the label on his jacket, with the word *'revenge'* – what could that mean?"

"Well, it could be any Nazi sympathizer, especially now that we know about this group and their protests."

Aaron then told the police officer about his threatening phone call.

"Please, sir, go to the police station and report this immediately! You must make a statement! As you are so well known, with good publicity someone might come forward and give us names – I'm sure of it."

"Yes, officer, we had planned to do that after visiting David, here."

"Well, I'll look out for you at the station. I must return there now; I've taken all the information I need from Mr. Koner here. Look after yourselves, please… and don't delay. See you later."

Andrew let the officer out, thanking him.

"Dave, you must stay with me and Gloria, until things settle down," said Aaron.

"Are you sure?"

"Absolutely; no question about it. As soon as you've packed some things, we'll go to the police station for me to make a statement, then we'll go home to Gloria. She doesn't know about any of this yet; I just hope she hasn't put the news on."

David packed enough for a few days and they locked the apartment up, making sure to set the alarm. They then made their way to the police station.

The officer who had spoken to them earlier was there, and took them into a room, where Aaron made a statement. Although Andrew and Aaron's secretary had searched the phone log, and found that the number had been withheld, the police officer said they had ways of tracing it; he just needed their telephone number, phone company account number and the name it was held in. So, Aaron rang the office and spoke to the secretary, who gathered all that information and sent it to the officer.

Once everything was in order, they made their way to Aaron's home, to tell Gloria what had happened. She obviously hadn't heard it on the news, or she would have been by now ringing Aaron in desperation.

"Sit down, darling; we've got some bad news," said Aaron.

David started to tell Gloria, but ended up sobbing. Andrew took over and gave her the full picture.

"Oh, my goodness! This is awful!" said Gloria. She grabbed hold of David and hugged him, as he sobbed on her shoulder.

"Dave, you must stay as long as you like," she said.

"It's going to make the news again tonight," warned Andrew. "There will be a full investigation. The police think it's linked to the Beiker case."

"Oh, dear," Gloria looked knowingly at Aaron, "I thought it might be."

"Dave, there is so much to do," said Andrew. "We'll be here to help you organize the funeral, and everything else that needs attending to."

"Well, the body can't be released yet, until the coroner has given permission."

"Let's just take one step at a time."

Later that evening, the national news reported it as a "hate crime", and went into detail about the possibility of a link to the Beiker case. They drew attention to "Britannica Yes", and their recent demonstrations against Jews and blacks. All in all, it was a good report, and the chief superintendent who delivered it was hopeful that they could solve the case.

"I need a gin," said David.

"Don't we all," said Gloria. "I'll do the honours."

Chapter 40

1993

BERLIN

IT TRANSPIRED THAT a neo-Nazi fanatic, who had known Beiker during the war, had followed his case intently, and had made contact with the group in Britain calling themselves "Britannica Yes". After months of investigations, the finger of suspicion pointed to this group, who it seemed had located Benjamin for this fanatical individual in Berlin.

But, while the group was only too keen to justify their beliefs, they wanted to distance themselves from Benjamin's murderer. They claimed that they were not anti-Semitic; they just wanted Britain to be free of immigrants, wherever they were from. To legitimize themselves, they betrayed neo-Nazi Ernst Schneider to the investigative authorities, and the police in Berlin quickly ascertained his whereabouts. When arrested, he was found to be in possession of copious Nazi memorabilia, just like Hans Beiker.

Following investigations into his lifestyle, there was overwhelming evidence that he had indeed committed Benjamin's murder. He was duly sentenced to life imprisonment.

Benjamin's funeral was Jewish, with all the rites and ceremonies traditional to an orthodox burial, even though he had denounced his faith. After the service in the synagogue, he was buried in the East Ham Jewish Cemetery, in London.

All the family attended and supported David, who was inconsolable. Due to the high profile of Aaron and Jack's charities, there was much publicity regarding Benjamin's murder and subsequent funeral. This drew many people to the funeral, to pay their respects, many of them people who had been helped by the two charities. Together with a sizeable portion of the Jewish community, there was a large number of mourners in attendance. It was a fitting tribute to one who had suffered so much in his early years.

The "family", of course, were not blood relatives; his real family had all perished under the Nazis. But Jack, Aaron, Gloria, Andrew, Joe, Clare, Jose and Alma, together with David, all considered themselves to be Benjamin's family, and they were all there to pray for the repose of his soul.

Afterward, they all went to the Hilton Hotel for a reception, to greet the rest of the mourners and to pay tribute to Benjamin.

Chapter 41

1993

BARCELONA

LATER THAT YEAR, another funeral took place in Barcelona: that of Señora Gabriella Sanchez, José's adoptive mother. It was held in the famous, still unfinished cathedral in Barcelona, where she had worshipped faithfully all her life, with her husband Miguel. It was where José had been baptized and served as an altar boy.

José, Alma and their daughter Lucia, together with Antonio, attended the funeral, as they promised they would. After their last of several visits, earlier in the year, Gabriella had slowly deteriorated. Given a new lease of life by having them back in her life, she had put up a braver fight than anyone had expected. Miguel had assured them that she was so much at peace now, and greatly comforted by José's visits with his family. They had made her last days easier to bear; she had been delighted to know that José was happily married to Alma, with a delightful little daughter. In the end, she had passed away peacefully.

The priest who had sold José to them had long since died. When Gabriella received viaticum on her deathbed, she poured her heart out to the young priest who ministered to her. She explained everything to him – the whole sordid story. However, she declared that she now felt no bitterness toward the Church, or for José and his father Antonio. The young priest was aghast at what she told him; being so young, he had only vague ideas of the turmoil of the history of the Church, and the dictatorship under which they lived. The civil war was not talked about, as shameful a part of Spain's history as it was.

So, Gabriella made her confession to the priest, and very soon afterward fell asleep and never awoke. It was a blissful end to a life which had been troubled health-wise and, particularly of late, emotionally.

The funeral Mass was very moving. José was still riddled with guilt, for his rejection of Gabriella and Miguel in the past. He was deeply moved during the ceremony, but with Antonio and Alma on each side of him, taking hold of his hands, they gave him strength.

After the funeral, everyone gathered in a local hotel for a reception. There were family members of Gabriella and Miguel present, as well as friends and neighbours in attendance, together with many fellow worshippers from the cathedral, who knew the family so well. Of course, José knew most of them. Wondering what they thought of him made him feel even more guilty.

Chapter 42

1980

LONDON

SEVERAL YEARS BEFORE, at one of Jack's most worrying times of life, the phone rang at the charity; Josie buzzed through to Jack's office.

"It's Dave Middleton for you, Jack."

It was what he had been waiting for. He took a deep, apprehensive breath. "Okay, Josie, put him through."

Another deep breath.

"Hey, Jack, it's Dave here. I need to see you, asap; I have some important news for you, but I don't want to speak over the phone."

"Okay, Dave, that's alright. Do you want to come to the office or the house?"

"How are you fixed this afternoon?"

"Okay, I think."

"Well, if it's alright I'll come to the office, about two-thirty."

"That's fine. I'll see you then."

Jack put the phone down, tortured and intrigued. He hoped – prayed – it was good news.

He couldn't eat his lunch; his stomach was churning at the thought of any more bad news. After a failed attempt, he tried to keep himself busy, but couldn't concentrate on anything.

He called Andrew, to see if he could pop over. He wanted him to hear whatever it was Dave had come back with.

Andrew had to make a few adjustments to his afternoon commitments, but arrived promptly at 2.20 p.m., and together they waited for Dave.

On the dot of 2.30 p.m., Josie buzzed through to say that Dave had arrived, and sent him in.

"Hi, both. I won't beat about the bush: it's good news! The man impersonating Hank Johnson has been arrested! His real name is

Clint Truman. He is wanted in the States for various crimes relating to fraud."

The two men gasped and cheered.

"Oh, thank God!" said Andrew, with tears in his eyes. "What a relief!"

"How did you find all this out, Dave?" said Jack, his voice shaking with elation.

"Well, you may remember my telling you that, as he had come from the States, entering this country would be a bit more complicated than coming from Europe; passport checks are more thorough. So, I put out an alert with my old department and one of my colleagues did some research: he found out that Hank Johnson actually died about five years ago!"

"Wow!"

"Clint Truman did serve with the G.I.s in Cardiff, and was part of a gang of lads who regularly met up with the local girls; he knew both Hank and Myra very well, so his story was easy to make up."

"How did he know there was money to be had?" said Jack.

"Come on, Jack; both the Blake Charity Foundation and Aaron's charity are famous. You're all practically celebrities!"

"Well, at least that's one thing less to worry about," said Jack.

"What a burden lifted!" said Andrew. "One father is more than enough to put up with!"

They all laughed, but the relief was tangible; the emotional turmoil "Hank" caused had been agony.

Dave went on to say that Clint Truman had been deported back to the States and arrested for several crimes. He was not going to cause trouble for anyone for quite some time.

Jack immediately rang Joe and Clare to put them out of their misery. They were hugely relieved.

Chapter 43

2004

LONDON

ANDREW LOOKED AT his mobile phone, where he saw a text from his Auntie Clare, which read:

"Andrew, your phone must have been on silent when I tried to ring you. Your dad's in hospital: St. Mary's, Paddington. Ring me please!"

In a panic, he rang Clare immediately.

"Auntie Clare, I was with a client. What's happened?"

"Your dad's had a heart attack. He's in coronary care."

Andrew felt like he'd been punched in the gut. "Is it bad?"

"Not looking good, Andrew. You need to get here as soon as you can."

"I'm on my way."

Clare and Joe met Andrew in the foyer, and he could immediately see that something was wrong.

"I'm sorry, Andrew, he's gone," said Joe.

"Oh, no," Andrew gasped. "I came as quickly as I could."

He fell into Clare's arms, sobbing. She consoled him and they sat down.

After a while, a nurse came over and said: "Would you like to see your father?"

"Yes, please. Can my aunt and uncle come with me?"

"Yes, of course. Follow me."

They made their way to the ward. When they got there the sister took over and led the three of them inside.

"Would you like me to call the chaplain?" asked the sister.

"Yes, please. That would be wonderful," said a tearful Andrew.

Jack was in a private room, and after the sister and the nurse had left them, Andrew closed the door. Andrew went to the bed and leaned over to kiss his father's forehead.

"I'm sorry, Dad," he said. "Sorry that I lived half my life without us knowing each other, as father and son. So many years were lost… wasted, because of my mother. But I've grown to love you so much in the time I have known you; you have more than made up for those lost years. No one could have had a better father! You are such a kind, generous, loving man, putting yourself last and others first – especially those in need."

He started to cry again, and Clare caught hold of him and squeezed his shoulders.

Just then, the hospital chaplain knocked on the door and came in.

"Hello, I'm Father Barry. I'm so sorry to hear your sad news, and to meet you under these circumstances. Please accept my deepest sympathy. I have come prepared to offer the customary prayers after death, if it is your wish."

"Yes, please, that would be wonderful. My dad was a man of faith, and has worshipped regularly all his life," said Andrew.

"That's wonderful to hear. Would you all please gather around the bed, and I'll begin?"

Joe, Clare and Andrew gathered around the bedside and held hands, as Father Barry began the customary prayers.

After he was done, Andrew shook his hand. "Thank you, Father. My dad would be so pleased to know you have done this."

"Would you like me to contact his parish priest, or will you do that yourselves?"

"We'll do it. Only last week he attended Mass; it was my mother's year's mind, and her name was mentioned in the intercessions for the deceased."

"That's fine. If I can be of any help just get in touch with the hospital here, and they will get hold of me."

"Thank you so much."

They shook hands again and Father Barry left them.

"I can't believe this has happened," said Andrew; "he seemed fine last week."

"I know," said Joe, "it's awful. I loved him as a brother, not a brother-in-law – especially after Myra's behaviour. I will miss him so much."

"We all will," said Clare.

"Well, we'd better set things in motion... start making funeral arrangements, and all that which needs to be done. I'm not sure what we should do first," said Andrew, a little bewildered.

"We'll help you with everything, Andrew. Let's just get home first, and we can make a list of things to do. We need to tell Aaron and his family... and David. They are all family, after all," said Joe.

They decided that Andrew should stay for a while at Joe and Clare's house, so they called in at his on the way, for him to pack a few things, before making their way there. Once they had settled him into one of the guest rooms, they started to make a list of things which needed attention. Top of the list was to call Aaron and José.

"Oh, my god," said Aaron, upon hearing the news. Through tears, he said: "I wouldn't be where I am today if it wasn't for you and Jack. He's been like a father to me."

"He was a legend," said Joe. "We'll catch up with you later, when we've made a few arrangements. Do you want to come over later?"

"Yes, that would be good. How is Andrew?"

"He's very tearful, but he will want to see you and José. I'm going to ring José now. He's in Spain, but I'm sure he will want to be here."

"Oh, no!" said José, when Joe called. "He has treated me like a son all these years. I can't believe it! How has Andrew taken it?"

"He's holding up. Aaron is coming over tonight, and we can make some arrangements."

"I'm going to book flights right now – and I'm sure Papá will come with me."

Joe put the phone down and decided he had better ring David as well – he was, after all, very much a part of this extraordinary extended family.

Meanwhile, Andrew contacted his father's parish priest, and asked if it was possible for Father Brian from Manchester to take part in the funeral, if he was able to attend. Father John gladly gave permission, and said that he would contact Father Brian to sort everything out. He promised to call the next day, to plan the order of service, hymns and eulogy, etc.

Two days later, Jose, Antonio, Alma and Lucia arrived, and stayed in Andrew's house.

The whole family made plans to meet up at Clare and Joe's house, to finalize the arrangements. It was going to be a big funeral.

Chapter 44

2004

LONDON

IT WAS INDEED a very big funeral.

It was held in St. Paul's Church, where Jack had worshipped, together with Joe and Clare, since he had moved to London to live.

The church was packed. There were representatives from the Charities Commission and other charitable organizations, as well as local councillors and even the local M.P. Many of the people Jack and Aaron had helped with housing and counselling were in attendance, and there were also representatives from the Housing Association, who had worked closely with Jack. The normal congregation of St. Paul's had also turned out in force, as they all adored Jack.

The "family" sat in the front pew, and consisted of Andrew, Joe, Clare, José, Alma, Lucia, Antonio, Aaron, Gloria, Rueben and David. Behind them sat Gloria's parents, Stephanie and David Bramwell, together with Mateo and Sonia Martinez, who had travelled from Spain out of respect for Jack – and, of course, José.

The funeral Mass was conducted with great dignity by Father John, who concelebrated with Father Brian. The main eulogy was delivered by Father Brian, who had known Jack since he was a boy; they had known each other in school, long before Brian took Holy Orders. He was able to give a perfect picture of Jack's selfless life without canonizing him. Andrew and Aaron also paid tribute, but they both struggled to speak about a man who had changed their lives.

The interment took place at Fulham Road Cemetery. It was announced in church that only the family were expected to attend this, so after the service everyone else made their way straight to the reception, being held at the Bulgari Hotel in Knightsbridge. Drinks were served to the mourners as they awaited the arrival of the family.

After the interment, the funeral cars brought the family and both priests to the Bulgari Hotel. It took quite some time for the family to greet everyone, and to listen to friends and acquaintances offer their condolences.

David kept Lucia and Rueben company, and they found a table in the corner of the reception room. They were obviously upset, though they didn't really know Jack as well as the others; there wasn't that emotional connection with past events, and they certainly didn't know any of the bigwigs who had turned up to support the family. Because of this, David stayed in their company until it was time to leave.

Aaron noticed a woman staring at him, and he was slightly perturbed. She was vaguely familiar. But there were hordes of people he wanted to shake hands with and chat to briefly, before he reached her. Still, every time he looked at her, he was drawn to her. Who was she? Eventually, Aaron caught up with the woman, who was making eye contact with him the whole time. He held his hand out to shake hers.

"Hello, I'm Aaron Goldberg. I don't think we've met… but your face is very familiar."

"Hello, Aaron." She took his hand, smiling. "Yes, we have met: I'm Rachel. I'm your sister."

Silence…

Aaron's eyes started to burn…

"You… you can't be…! She perished in Auschwitz, along with my mother and father…"

But she just smiled and shook her head.

Was this a trick? Had neo-Nazis caught up with him? Or maybe the Soviet K.G.B.? She had a vague Russian accent!

Aaron looked more closely, and the familiarity gradually became much clearer, like fog dissipating. And soon he could see an older version of his sister staring back at him. It was like looking at his mother! God, it was no wonder he felt that she was so familiar. He didn't know whether to cry, hug her or flee!

"Aaron, is there somewhere we can talk?"

Silence. She looked at him questioningly.

"Y… yes. Yes! We can go to one of the rooms through there," he pointed to a doorway, suddenly perking up.

Gloria saw him walking toward the door with the strange woman, and wondered what was going on. *It must be business,* she thought. But how rude, to come to a funeral and expect him to deal with work, at a time like this.

Once they were settled in a small, adjoining room, Aaron said to her: "Are you really Rachel Goldberg?"

"Yes, I am. On the platform, when we were herded off of the cattle trucks, you and Papa were selected for work; Mama and I were herded with everyone else toward a huge, underground bunker. In there, we were told to undress, ready for a shower. It was ghastly! All of those thuggish S.S. brutes were watching and sniggering. One of them caught my eye and I quickly looked away, but he came up and started to look at me. Then, he shouted a command at one of the woman guards, who quickly came over with my clothes and told me to get dressed. I was terrified of what was going to happen to me. Mama started crying, too, and she was slapped hard by one of the woman guards."

Aaron knew straight away, from her description, that she was telling the truth; this was exactly how it had happened. She even accurately described the brute who had clubbed her father, when he asked if Aaron could work with him.

"Oh, Rachel! It's you! It's really you!"

They embraced and sobbed loudly.

"What happened to you? How did you survive?"

"I was taken to another part of the camp, called Birkenau. There were large warehouses there, where all the belongings stolen from the inmates were stored. It was nicknamed 'Canada', because it was a place of abundance."

"Canada?" said Aaron.

"Yes. Ironic, isn't it? In a place where everyone was starved to death, there was a place named for its abundance!"

"So, what happened there?"

"We had to sort shoes, clothing, suitcases, photographs,

jewellery... everything that people had brought with them. The Nazis were very cunning; as you know, they told everyone – just like we were told – to pack valuable and important items, and nothing else. This meant that there were a lot of valuable items for them to help themselves to."

"Bastards! What happened to these items?"

"They were shipped off to Germany and sold to people there, to help boost the coffers of the Third Reich!"

"Now that the Third Reich is dead and buried, I wonder what has happened to all that gold. What were the conditions like there?"

"They were rather better than what you and Papa had to endure; we were fed better food, to keep us fit enough to do the work. Once there, we would not have contact with any other areas in the camp; it was almost like a secret place, even though we all knew what was going on.

"When I was released, I quickly learned the fate of our dear mother."

"Why didn't you try to see if Papa or I had survived, and find us?"

"I did try, Aaron. After we were liberated, I went through the process that you probably had to go through, and eventually I was given a *Certificate of Liberation*. Before going home, I went to the Restitutional Offices in Berlin, only to be told that you had both perished."

Aaron wasn't surprised. "Are you married? Do you have a family?"

"I was married, to a good man. He was Russian – that's where I have lived for all of these years. He died of cancer some time ago. It was odd living under Soviet rule, but nothing as bad as the Nazis! Even so, because of the Cold War, information from the West was stilted. It is only recently that news has infiltrated."

"I'm sorry you lost your husband. Have you got children?"

"Ye—"

Just then, Gloria came into the room. "Aaron, everyone is wondering where you've got to. Who is this?"

Aaron explained that Rachel was his sister, who had survived the Holocaust.

Gloria was stunned – and delighted.

"Oh, my god! How wonderful! This is truly amazing!" blurted Gloria, and the siblings laughed. She came closer and shook hands with Rachel.

"I can see the likeness! Come, we must tell everyone; this is absolutely fantastic news!"

"I'm sorry I slipped off, but Rachel was looking at me during the reception and I felt drawn to her; I seemed to know her face somehow! I can't believe my little sister is still alive!"

"Come on. This is cause for celebration, even on this sad day! Jack would be over the moon!"

They returned to the reception, in time to see Andrew making a speech, to pay tribute to his father. Glasses were raised and a toast was made to Jack.

Then, just as Andrew was about to tell everyone that the buffet was ready, Gloria stood next to him and whispered something in his ear. He raised his eyes and looked directly at Aaron and Rachel, with an astonished look on his face.

Aaron smiled and mouthed: "It's really her!"

Gloria cleared her throat and said: "Dear friends, on this sad day, when we have all lost someone very special to us – a dear father, brother and friend – Jack would be delighted to know what I am about to tell you. You all know Aaron's background, and the terrible things he has been through in his youth. Well, today we can raise our glasses again, with Jack's approval, because it turns out that Aaron's sister Rachel survived the horrors of Auschwitz, and she is here with us today."

Gasps all around…

Aaron brought Rachel to the forefront, and everyone clapped and cheered.

Andrew said: "My father would be so happy to hear this wonderful news! So, with him watching over us, let's raise a glass to Rachel Goldberg – and to survival!"

Glasses clinked, along with more cheers and clapping.

Aaron and Rachel then spent some time shaking hands with people. He introduced her to many friends and acquaintances.

Eventually, the mourners started to drift away, and only the family were left.

Andrew chatted with Rachel, and introduced her to Joe, Clare and the rest of the family. "And, of course, this is your nephew Rueben – named after your father, I believe."

"Oh, my goodness; he looks just like him!" At this, she started to cry.

Andrew held her tight. "You have a new, international family now, Rachel. We're a mixed bag, but we're a family. Very cosmopolitan."

Aaron came over and hugged her, too.

"Well, everyone," said Andrew, "let's go back to my dad's house, where we can get better acquainted with Rachel. She must have lots to tell us. And we certainly have a great deal to explain to her!"

EPILOGUE

THEY ALL GATHERED at Jack's home, where Madge had prepared a sumptuous meal for them all, having slipped off early during the reception to make preparations.

Rachel was astonished at the stories that Aaron, Andrew, José and David told her. She, in turn, told them all about "Canada".

"So, Rachel, you've told us that your husband died of cancer, which is very sad. You also said you have a son. Tell us about him."

"Well, Jack actually met him some years ago, when he was making enquiries about you, Aaron!"

"What?!"

"His name is Ivan Steningrav. He works at the Russian embassy, here in London. He met Jack with a man from the bank in Manchester: George Stanhope. Ivan couldn't be sure of his facts, but he knew that my maiden name was Goldberg. Still, because of the Cold War, it took some time to clarify everything and to get Aaron released. However, he was obstructed from getting this news to me by some K.G.B. officer, who was suspicious that there was something more going on – you know all about the Soviets and their behaviour, I'm sure."

"That's astonishing," said Andrew.

"Well, my husband – Nikita Steningrav – had died by this time, otherwise he might have looked into this further, as he worked for the government. In fact, he was responsible for getting Ivan his job here at the Russian embassy. It was only when glasnost and perestroika happened that Ivan was able to delve deeper into the mystery, and eventually contacted me in confidence that he wouldn't be apprehended."

"Oh, my goodness; what an incredible turn of events! Where is he now? We must meet him! He's part of this mixed bag of a family, too," said David.

"Well, he came to church for the funeral with me, but had to dash back to the embassy for an appointment. I'm going to ring him now, if that's alright, and give him directions to join us here."

*

Later, Ivan arrived, and it seemed that the family was complete.

Fathers and sons together had created a unique story, with a band of people who were bound together by circumstances and the benevolence of charity.

There were Jack and Andrew, Rueben and Aaron, Antonio and José, even Nikita and Ivan… but none could have done what they did without the help of so many others – especially the women in their lives.

Acknowledgements

The publisher would like to thank Russell Spencer, Matt Vidler, Laura-Jayne Humphrey, Lianne Bailey-Woodward, Leonard West and Susan Woodard for their hard work and efforts in making this published book a reality.

The publisher would also like to thank Robert Donkin for allowing them to publish their work.

The author would like to thank L.R. Price Publications Ltd for their confidence in them and therefore publishing this book and also their previous book.

"I've learned much from the laid back lifestyle in Spain and the inspiration it has given me.

I thank the Holocaust Memorial Society for the information that inspired me to write about Aaron Goldberg.

It was internet searching that provided the information to write about the Niños Robados as well as television dramas regarding the scandal. War records provided the information I needed regarding the bombing of Cardiff." - Robert Donkin

About the Publisher

LR Price Publications is dedicated to publishing books by unknown authors.

We use a mixture of traditional and modern publishing methods to bring our authors' words to the wider world.

We print, publish, distribute and market books in a variety of formats including paper and hard back, electronic books e-books, digital audio books and online.

If you are an author interested in getting your book published; or a book retailer interested in selling our books, please contact us.

www.lrpricepublications.com

L.R. Price Publications Ltd,
27 Old Gloucester Street,
London, WC1N 3AX.

(0203) 051 9572

publishing@lrprice.com

About the Author

"I was born in Neath, South Wales and wondered, until I was about eight years old, why I didn't have a father until my mother plucked up the courage to tell me that he had deserted us and didn't want to have anything to do with me.

This has haunted me for most of my life.

After working in a Steel Works for three years I offered myself for Ordination to the Priesthood in the Anglican Church. Many varied and interesting incidents in my life as a priest are recorded in my first book – A Time To Weep and a Time to Laugh.

I am married with two grown up children and three grandchildren.

Since retirement my wife and I spend six months of the year in our apartment in Spain. Life there has inspired the Spanish connection in this book."

-Robert Donkin

www.ingramcontent.com/pod-product-compliance
Lightning Source LLC
LaVergne TN
LVHW020043110826
845155LV00029B/613
* 9 7 8 1 9 1 6 8 8 7 4 5 9 *